AF436580

Veronica

Asif Hossain

Published by

Turquoise Book House 2023

Copyright © 2023 Asif Hossain

Cover Artwork © Darren Thompson

Cover Design © Natalia Ivanonva

All rights reserved.

ISBN 9789843549020

Turquoise Book House

Dedication

For my friend Mishu, who was a precious soul. Who was a better fighter than any of us. It rained heavily the day you passed away. You always hated the rain for some reason. I guess I agree with you now. I hope you remember how we always smoked at your place and how you complained about all of your stuff while we listened. I sometimes thought, Oh, she talks a lot. Now I think, if I could turn back time, I would just let you talk and never utter a word again. Now that you've left us, who do you complain to? Maybe you don't have too much to complain about anymore. I hope you're happy and free now, watching us from somewhere over the rainbow.

Contents

"When I was younger I thought if I could leave home, pay rent, and feed myself, I would become an adult. If I became an adult I thought I wouldn't have to cry anymore. I'm even terrible at depression. I am a cuckoo, standing on top of the lives that were pushed aside. As they sing of spring, I hear a voice calling in the distance and I think, if I ever really were a bird, then at least I would pass through the days oblivious to such agonizing torment as this."

--3月はライオンのようにやってくる (March comes in like a lion, 2007) by Chica Umino

CHAPTER ONE

L-I-V-I-N

On a remarkably calm mid-June day, the sun's scorching heat gradually warmed the earth in its customary fashion. Veronica found herself engrossed in the pages of a thick paperback, reclining on the grass. The usual crowd that frequented this place during the afternoon was conspicuously absent; the sweltering mid-day temperatures dissuaded anyone from venturing out into the open sun. However, Veronica was an exception. She cherished this time of day above all others precisely because of its solitude and emptiness. She had carefully propped up an umbrella, providing her with much-needed shade from the relentless sun. Beneath its shelter, she immersed herself in her own world of words and thoughts.

Veronica spent her formative years in a small neighborhood that, in her eyes, lacked any semblance of excitement. Disdain for this place simmered within her; she found the people around her to be unappealing and devoid of intrigue. As a result, she refrained from socializing much, even with her closest friend from class, who seemed to engage with her less frequently. The notion that she belonged to the wrong era weighed heavily on her mind. Listening to her grandmother's stories, she couldn't help but yearn for the bygone days of yore. According to her grandmother, life in their generation brimmed with merriment and delight. School was a joyful experience, vacations were filled with fun adventures, and music resonated with a certain magic that she felt was absent in her own time. The reminiscences of midnight parties and electrifying Rock n' roll concerts captured her imagination, making her wistful for a world she never had the chance to experience. Once, she said, she and her friends went to an Aerosmith show, and on their way back, everyone was dead drunk. So they decided to shoplift at a convenience store just to have fun. The cashier got them bad and pulled out a shotgun; they drove like madmen to save themselves from that. She had a special relationship with her grandmother, a woman whose kind disposition and considerate nature won the hearts of all who knew her. She gave off a respectful aura that rendered her presence undetectable. She was a respected professor at a prestigious university during her prime, and at the age of 51, she gracefully ended her academic career. She then lost herself in the world of records and books. Tragically, her grandmother passed away six months prior, leaving behind a priceless collection of books and records that are now Veronica's property. On occasion, she would listen to the records her grandmother had cherished so much while digging through this treasure trove.

Veronica sets her book aside and stands up. After taking a quick look around, she picks up her book and places it inside her tote bag. She stands up, grabs her umbrella, and heads back home. She dislikes staying at home as well. She does not get along well with her parents. Her father is a professional lawyer. Her mother has a position with a business. Almost everything she wants to do in life is opposed by them. She doesn't give a damn, though. She is quiet and able to keep quiet even when she is extremely enraged. In her entire life, she has hardly ever yelled at anyone.

She takes her keys out of her bag and opens the door to her house. After taking off her shoes, she goes to the refrigerator and pulls out a soda can. Cracking it open, she takes a cool sip. She then makes her way up to the second floor and into her room. Next to her bed, a sizable poster of Phoebe Bridgers can be seen on the wall. Patti Smith's "M

Train," which she had been reading the night before, is on her table. The book was a gift from her grandmother. In the left corner of her room, a sturdy record shelf showcases her personal collection of vinyl records, along with those passed down from her grandmother. Not far from the record shelf stands a bookshelf, proudly displaying books of diverse genres. Her favorite book quotes and song lyrics are written on a few sticky notes that are hung on the wall in front of her table. She removes her bag, leaving it on the chair, then picks up the book from the table, returning it to the shelf. After turning on the air conditioner with the remote, Veronica eases off her socks and collapses onto her bed. She buries her face into the softness of the mattress, seemingly seeking relief from an overwhelming exhaustion.

"So what have you decided?" asks Veronica's father, breaking the customary silence at the dinner table. "What university are you applying to?"

It was a rare occasion when everyone in the family was seated together, and her father's question highlighted Veronica's upcoming choice regarding her future educational path.

"I don't know yet," Veronica replies.

"If you don't know now, when will you decide? This is a

critical moment in your life, and your choice will shape your future. Take your time, but make a thoughtful decision. James's daughter is going to Princeton next year. I want you to go somewhere better too."

She is not at all interested in the idea of attending college. She is preoccupied with her own world and lost in thought. One might argue that it is a careless approach to one's future, but one must ultimately live the life they choose. What is there to live for if one only pursues what other people want and never considers their own dream?

Coming to her defense, her mother interjects, "Give her some space. She just finished school, and she deserves time to think. Choosing a university is a significant step, and we should support her in finding the right path."

"Can I have her bike once she's away?" Veronica's brother chims in with a hint of sarcasm.

"Shut up," she retorts firmly, not amused by her brother's jest.

Her younger brother kevin is polar opposite to her in every way. He is talkative, outgoing, and full of energy. This year, he turned fifteen. He is also well-known among girls. Even a few of Veronica's classmates like him because of how good and charming he is with women. He adores films more than anything else. In his room, he has a poster for Richard Linklater's cult classic 'Dazed and Confused' from the 90s. That movie is his favourite. Veronica saw the movie on one occasion. She adored it as well, but not in the same way that he would have. She preferred watching arthouse films. However, some of the movie's dialogue has changed her perspective. For example when the character Wooderson played by Matthew Mcconaughey said, *"Man, it's the same bullshit they tried to pull in my day. If it ain't that piece of paper, there's some other choice they're gonna try and make for you. You gotta do what Randall 'Pink' Floyd wants to do, man. Let me tell you this: The older you do get, the more rules they're gonna try to get you to follow. You just gotta keep livin', man, L-I-V-I-N."* These lines made her think about life. She was deeply moved by the movie's strong message about being true to oneself and living life on one's terms. It caused her to consider whether she was truly living or merely following social conventions. In addition, the film revived memories of her grandmother's youth, creating a sense of connection and nostalgia. Her grandmother's account of her own experiences sounded exactly like the characters in the movie. She was comparing the carefree attitude of the movie's characters to the adventurous spirit of her grandmother.

As she lay in her room, absorbed in reading the latest release of Inside Out magazine, she hears a faint knock on her door. Putting the magazine aside, she gets up and walks over to open it. On the other side was her younger brother. Veronica sits on her bed and picks up the magazine on her hand again. Her brother sits in her chair in a comfortable position. He's wearing a Maneskin T-shirt. His long hair makes him look older than his age.

"Do you have some money you can lend me?" asks her brother.

"Shut up. I've got nothing I can spare. I'm saving up for something. Besides, where's the money I lent you last month?"

"What are you saving for? All you do is sit here and there and read books. You don't even go out."

"Because I like it." She says it as if she isn't at all offended by his comments.

Her relationship with her brother is exactly what typical siblings are like. Despite being different, they do help each other sometimes. She lets Kevin bring his girlfriends over while their parents are out at work. She doesn't care what they do.

"Why you need money anyway?" She asks.

"I've gotta buy a gift for Nancy. Her birthday is the day

after tomorrow."

"Who's Nancy? What about Denise? I thought you were dating Denise."

"Come on! You know I date several girls. Nancy is the new one."

"Well, you can go to hell with her. I can't help you this time. I'm Sorry."

"What are you saving up for anyway?" he asks as he gets up to leave the room.

"I'm going on a tour. I don't know where. But I'm gonna go soon. Maybe somewhere, I don't know. But I sure know that I wanna go and I'm going. And yeah, don't tell that to mom and dad. They're gonna be mad and think I've gone crazy. But I'm totally saying this in a normal state." She replies.

He chuckles mockingly and says, "Well, you do sound crazy to me now. I mean, you? Tour? Come on. It doesn't sound very realistic to me. If you said tomorrow our family's gonna move to Switzerland, it would have been more realistic than what you're saying, I guess."

Veronica understood what he meant. It was out of character for her to go on and do something like that. But she also realises she has seen only a little. She feels that even though she has lived many lives in the eyes of the characters in the books she reads, she has never lived her own. She never experienced life like she should. It's just like what's said in Dead Poets Society: *"That the powerful play goes on, and you may contribute a verse."* She thinks she hasn't contributed her verse. So it's high time she did. So the advice of her dad about choosing a university and her future was kept aside.

"I want to live in the present. I want to live today as if there is no tomorrow. I want to live so that even if I die tomorrow, I can tell the angel of death that I've lived a worthy life." She says to herself.

She worked incredibly hard that summer, taking on two part-time jobs. One was working as a McDonald's cashier, and the other was at a nearby amusement park's gift shop. It was difficult to juggle both schedules, but she persisted. She remained inspired throughout the long days thanks to her tenacity and strong sense of purpose. She persevered despite being exhausted because she was motivated by her goals. Her diligence paid off, and she was able to accumulate a sizeable sum of money. Her willingness to make sacrifices that summer was evidence of her dedication to achieving her objectives. She felt a sense of pride and satisfaction as she saw the results of her labour, knowing that her efforts had not gone in vain.

She decides to start her journey in October, when the landscape was painted with the vivid hues of the autumn. She had always had a special place in her heart for autumn, and something about the season's special charm seemed to speak to her. She was able to change and deepen her mood in response to the crispness of the air, the rustling of leaves underfoot, and the warm colours of autumn foliage. She prepared herself with necessities the day before.

"Are you going for sure?" asks her brother while she was packing her bags.

"No doubt about it; you can see."

"Damn, that's crazy."

"Well, what can I say? I'm just doing it, you know."

"Yeah, got it. You just gotta keep livin' man." he says, mimicking the accent of Wooderson, the character from "Dazed and Confused."

"L-I-V-I-N" she echoes as they both burst into laughter.

She informed her mother that she was going to stay at Grandma's house for a while. It's for a change, and after that, she'll choose the college she'll enrol in. Her mother believed that staying alone in a location where a deceased person's memories still lingered was a spooky idea. Yet she fell for her lies. Her mother reasoned that she might be missing her grandma so much because they were so close. She even gave her permission to take her car without hesitating and also handed over money to get it fueled up.

Veronica woke up early this morning. After saying goodbye to her parents, she gets to her room and checks if there's anything missing that she should pick up for her trip. She has taken a few books, clothes, her diary, a camera, and, of course, the money that she saved. As her mother gave her money to get the car fueled up, she now has some extra money to spare and thinks of her brother. She goes to her brother's room and sees that he is gone already. She notices two new posters: of Black Flag and Minor Threat. He must have somehow discovered the 80s punk scene, she thinks. She puts some money in an envelope and leaves it for him. She returned to her room and dressed herself in a comfortable cotton T-shirt and an olive-colored cardigan. Standing in front of the mirror, she began to brush her short hair, which fell gracefully over her shoulders. With her striking appearance, she was the kind of girl who would catch anyone's attention at first glance. Her beauty was undeniable, but she seemed uninterested in the boys who approached her. Instead, she found them somewhat off-putting. Inwardly, she questioned her feelings and inclinations, realising that she might be attracted to girls. Her moments of arousal often involved thoughts of women's bodies, further adding to her introspection about her own identity and preferences. However, she has always kept that to herself. There was no way she could talk about that with her conservative parents. She has never fell for anyone in particular yet. Back in middle school, she noticed that boys were approaching her quite frequently. But because of how cut off she was from other people, she remained single. Even if someone ever expresses interest in her, her actions show that she is uninterested. She doesn't care all that much, so they move on because of that.

She takes a bit of time to find any flaws in herself in the mirror. She takes her car keys and phone, but removes her SIM card. She sends a voice message to her mother before doing that, saying, "Hey mom, it's me. I'm heading towards Grandma's, and I'm unplugging my sim, just to have a break from everything else. You shouldn't be worrying about me; I'll be fine. I'll get back to you soon."

She puts the bag on her shoulder while the headphones hang on her neck, closes the door to her room, descends the stairs, and carefully locks the front door. keeping the keys hidden under the rug. She then makes her way to the car, places her bag on the back seat, and climbs into the driver's seat. She sees to it that her driver's licence is taken. To play music, she pairs her phone with the car's Bluetooth. She pulls a pack of cigarettes out of her pocket and lights one with the lighter that was probably her mother's that was kept in front. 'Farewell' by Bob Dylan begins to play as she presses the shuffle button on her playlist and starts the car while puffing on a cigarette.

CHAPTER TWO

Both Sides Now

She's driving through the streets as the scenarios pass her by. She has kept the window of the driver's seat wide open as she's smoking another cigarette. The autumn wind breezes through the window. She's driving at a steady speed. A blue Chevy Malibu just overtook her. Going at a speed as if it's a racing competition. But she didn't care about that much. She doesn't seem shocked by that speed either. She's calm, as she has always been. When she set out, she didn't have a specific destination in mind. Later, however, she began to have the urge to travel to the Ozarks. For some reason, when her brother inquired, she brought it up. Going to the Ozarks now seems like a viable option to her. Summertime sees the majority of tourists. However, now is probably the off-season. So it won't be a problem for her to stay there for a few days. The distance to her destination is long. And for her, that is the best aspect. She chooses to take detours that will require her to travel further than usual. She remembers a poem of Robert Frost while taking that decision. The last verses of 'The Road Not Taken':

> *"I shall be telling this with a sigh*
> *Somewhere ages and ages hence:*
> *Two roads diverged in a wood, and I—*
> *I took the one less traveled by,*
> *And that has made all the difference."*

Those words appeared to capture the essence of her present situation, where she was at a crossroads of her own. The decision she was about to make felt important, just like the one Frost had envisioned in his enduring verses.

Before hitting the highway that led through the woods, she notices a nearby super shop and decides to stop and get some supplies. Parking her car, she steps out, locks it, and tucks the keys into her jeans pocket before heading towards the store. Inside, she picks up a few cans of food and five cans of beer. Making her way to the counter, she paid for her items and swiftly left, ready to continue her journey with provisions in hand. She returns to her driving seat, starts the car, and continues driving. Once again, she keeps the window open, relishing the feeling of the air caressing her face and playing with her hair. Every aspect of this journey brings her joy, and she cherishes every thought that crosses her mind. It is as if she is the protagonist of a well-written novel, and the sense of freedom envelops her. Above all, she feels genuinely happy as she continues to drive along the open road.

It is just before sunset as she drives along the highway and notices a man, probably in his mid-20s, walking alongside the road near the woods with a backpack on his back. He sees her car approaching and signals for a lift. She observes him, passes by at a slow speed, and ponders for a moment. Finally, she decides to stop her car a few steps ahead. The man doesn't appear desperate, which is one of the reasons she considers helping him. Moreover, she hasn't seen many cars pass by on this road during her drive. If he genuinely needs assistance, he might be stranded alone on this path even after dark. Taking these factors into account, she decides to provide him a lift. She stops the music and opens the door, allowing the man to get in.

"Thanks," he says as he settles into the car.

Veronica remains silent, focusing on the road ahead. There's something peculiar about the man; he appears visibly upset, with a face that exudes deep melancholy. Dark circles under his eyes suggest a lack of proper sleep for a long time, and his eyes seem hollow and distant.

"Where do you want me to drop you off?" Veronica asks, breaking the silence.

"Oh, yeah, I'll get off at the next right turn," the man responds, as if he had been lost in deep thought and only returned to reality after her question.

A sudden strange fear grips her. What if there's a potential risk from the man? What if he suddenly tries to attack her? The remote location and the lack of nearby help intensify her nervousness. Breaking the silence, she decides to assert herself, hoping to deter any potential threat. About them, she had heard tales. Frequently, and sometimes worse, people are killed in the woods. When she let the man in, she didn't consider it. However, her thoughts begin to shift now that he is there. One of those obtrusive thoughts that can make a person second-guess their choice.

"Just so you know, I've got a Glock 19 on me, fully loaded. So you better think twice before trying anything," she says, pretending to be the one he should be afraid of if he has any ill intentions.

"You'd be doing me a favor if you shoot me with it," the man replies, his gaze fixed ahead.

Her heart sinks as she instantly regrets her words. The man just gave her an utterly depressing response. She was aware that some people experienced depression and had suicidal thoughts, but she had never personally encountered one. This man sounds exactly like one, and given the situation, she can infer that he may have even tried to commit suicide at least once. Her previous ideas, which she had before hearing what he said, start to shift once more. Once again, silence fills the space between them, and the uneasiness in the car becomes palpable.

She hasn't been in contact with a person like this before. By his tone and looks, and after what he just said, it has been clear to her that he's probably been through a lot. She feels a little bit eager to know what's going on with him, but she decides not to talk. The man still has his gaze fixated on the road; sometimes he's looking out the side of his window, but not once has he looked towards her.

"You know," the man says, turning his gaze towards the window beside him, "you shouldn't have told me about the gun, especially in these circumstances. You should never reveal your cards to someone if you perceive them as a potential risk."

"I regret saying that," Veronica replies calmly.

"Regret won't mean anything if you lose your life over something like that," he responds.

Veronica falls silent once more, contemplating his words. There's something about the way he speaks that touches her. His voice sounds lost and empty, like an old man who has lost his way and is only waiting for death to arrive. In his words, she senses a profound sadness, and her heart aches for the burdens he carries. She still has no idea what happened to him. She is curious, but she is hesitant to confront him about it. She has spent almost her entire life doing this. Putting off doing what she really wants to do. But at least now that she is travelling, she is taking action.

"What were you doing here anyway?" she asks.

"I was camping. In the forest," he replies.

"Alone?"

"Yeah."

"How did that go?"

"Usual."

"Usual? You do that often?"

"Yeah." This time, he takes a glance at her.

"Do you like it?"

"I don't like anything except nature."

She doesn't press further with questions, sensing that he lost himself long ago. Despite his past trauma or grief, he continues to find solace in the woods, perhaps the only thing that keeps him grounded, even if only temporarily.

"You ever wondered," he says, pausing briefly, "that trees and rocks can talk to humans too?"

"No. Never," she responds. While knowing it isn't possible, she refrains from inquiring further about how or why, sensing that he will share regardless.

"Well, they do. If you listen closely and pay attention, you can hear them too. But the catch is, you can only hear them when you are surrounded by them and have had no contact with other humans or animals."

"So, what did they tell you this time?"

"They told me that these woods are for living. If I want to save myself, I should lose myself among the leaves, in the mud I step on, and in the breeze that touches my skin. And they will bless me with rain to soothe my heart."

She found the words to be visibly strange. She has encountered many oddballs throughout elementary and high school. Perhaps some might think of her as a weird person. But she is aware of who she was. She was certain that she wasn't weird just because she didn't like to talk to people very much. What about the man, though? Is he truly sane, or has he gone insane? Does what he's saying make any sense at all? She thinks that the reason people are labelled as crazy or insane is because everyone else does not understand what they mean or see. In some ways, she believed that the insane knew more than the average person.

She drops him off as the sun has fully set, leaving behind a sky adorned with glowing rays. The car continues its journey through the twilight, and the man steps forward on his own, lost in his thoughts. As he walks away, she decides to note down what he said about the woods speaking to humans. She stops the car for a moment, retrieves her diary, and writes down his words exactly as he spoke them: *"These woods are for living. If I want to save myself, I should lose myself among the leaves, in the mud I step on, and in the breeze that touches my skin. And they will bless me with rain to soothe my heart."*

It was dark sooner than she expected, and she decides it's best not to drive at night. Consulting her phone's maps, she searches for a nearby motel to spend the night. After a few kilometres, she locates one. Situated in the surrounding landscape, it appears to be the only establishment in the area. The motel stands as a modest structure, its exterior bathed in a dim glow from the few scattered lamps. Its weathered facade tells tales of time passed, and the flickering lights create a sense of mystery in the stillness of the night. The parking lot is sparsely occupied, and the occasional sound of crickets fills the air. As she approaches the reception area, a neon sign flickers, casting an eerie aura over the entrance. When Veronica gets close to the counter, she notices a middle-aged woman there talking on the phone. There are no other people visible on that floor, and the reception area is quiet. But she noticed two cars parked outside, suggesting that the motel probably has a few visitors staying there. Trying not to interrupt the woman's phone call, she waits patiently. It has an unsettling feeling like the motel is a place frozen in time, unaffected by the outside world. The only sounds that break the silence are a faint hum from the air conditioner and a sporadic creak from the floorboards.

Finally, the woman finishes her call and looks up, offering Veronica a warm smile. "Welcome to Sunset Motel. How can I help you tonight?" she asks in a friendly tone.

She requests a room for the night. The woman checks the availability and hands her a key. "Room 205, second floor, on your left," she says, pointing down the hallway.

She takes the key and heads towards her room, eager to rest after a long day on the road.

When Veronica reaches the second floor, she notices four rooms on each side of the hallway. The motel has only three floors, and there's still no sign of any other humans on this floor, leading her to assume that the other guests must be on the third floor. She walks down the hallway towards room

205 and inserts her key into the lock, unlocking the door. As she enters, she sees the bathroom on the right side of the room. The space inside is narrow, with just a few metres between the entrance and the main area of the room. The room itself is simple but cozy, with a comfortable bed, a small table with a lamp, and a dresser. She sits on the bed and turns on the lamp. A soft glow from the lamp illuminates the room. Veronica takes a moment to settle in, placing her bag on the dresser and her diary on the bedside table. She glances out the window, where the moonlight softly filters through the curtains, creating shadows on the floor.

She takes a deep, long breath and throws herself on the bed. After lying down for a few minutes, she gets up and opens up a can of food from her bag. But she doesn't feel like eating that one. She feels as if she's going to throw up if she eats that now. So she doesn't eat it and leaves it in the bin. She goes to the bathroom and splashes water on her face. After getting out, she takes off her cardigan and t-shirt, replacing them with another comfortable t-shirt that had a nice photo of a sakure tree printed on it; below the print, the word "Sakura" is written in Japanese letters.

She closes the door and makes her way down the corridor. The hallway's lighting is incredibly dim. A faint sound coming from room 209 leads her to believe there is likely another person on the floor. She descends to the first floor using the stairs. It appears that the woman is still on the phone with someone. She has a low voice while speaking. If she spoke louder, the atmosphere in the motel would have caused her voice to at least travel down the second-floor hallway. Veronica patiently waits for the woman's phone call to end while she sits on the sofa in front of the counter. It is incredibly quiet here. With an incredibly soft voice, the woman is talking on the phone. However, if one listens closely, it can be heard at a fair distance.

Finally, the woman finishes her call, and with a smile, she turns her attention to Veronica. "I apologise for the wait. How can I assist you?" she asks politely.

"I was wondering if there are any restaurants nearby. Do you know where I can find one?"

"There's one. Go straight down the main road and take the left. Go straight again, and you will see a narrow path on the right that leads to a café."

"Thanks." She said so and got up.

She leaves the motel and stands outside, contemplating whether to walk or take her car. After a moment of consideration, she decides that driving would be safer in the darkness of the night. Veronica unlocks her car door, settles into the driver's seat, and starts the engine. She turns on the headlights and begins to drive. As she pulls out of the motel parking lot, she notices that the two other cars that were parked there earlier are still in their places. The road ahead stretches out in front of her, shrouded in the cloak of the night. The night seems dark and there isn't even lampposts around. She never thought she will come across such distant place all by herself someday. She reads a lot and has come across tales about characters wandering alone on eerie nights. Now that she is in the situation by herself, she is able to experience it firsthand. Life is all about feelings, she thinks. Sometimes, even the pain itself has great significance. People who are not feeling are not really living. To feel again, they can exchange anything. Not just a feeling of happiness, but also of rage, melancholy, and pain. There is no distinction between a dead man and a person who is still alive but has no emotion.

She reaches the road that leads to the café in a few minutes. However, the road is too narrow for her car to pass through. Reluctantly, she parks the car by the side and continues on foot. As she approaches the café, she notices its old-fashioned architecture, with a weathered wooden exterior and a small sign hanging above the entrance. Dimly lit lanterns line the pathway, casting a glow on the surroundings. She steps through the wooden door into the café. As she enters the café, Veronica notices two men sitting at the main counter table, engaged in conversation with the attendant as they enjoy their drinks. The seating arrangements extend horizontally on both sides of the entrance. Apart from the two men at the counter, there's only one elderly gentleman seated at the far end of the left corner. "Laura" by Charlie Parker was playing inside the café. As she enters, everyone seems to take a glance at her. She sits in the right corner. The ambience is reminiscent of the 1950s thanks to the jazz music playing. Everything about this place seems a little dated, including the architecture of the cafe and the people. She almost has the impression that she is going back in time. A waitress approaches her and takes her order. She orders a peach pie and black coffee. She takes a paperback out of her bag and starts reading.

The waitress approaches with her order as Veronica flips a page from her paperback. Keeping the peach pie aside, she seems more interested in taking a sip of the coffee. The atmosphere of the café is still the same. Only the music has changed a few times.

A young man and a woman walk through the door a short

while later. This time, everyone looks their way, including Veronica, as they cast a glance. They were talking about selling some property or something, and they were a little noisy. The thought of being loud in a public place feels like a nightmare to her. All her life, she has been quiet, even to herself. But how can these people be loud to others? She wonders. The old man casts a longer-than-normal glance at the couple as he turns to face them from the corner. The wrinkles are visible on his face. He is wearing a thick frame. The music shifts to Doris Day's version of "Dream a little dream of me."

Veronica finishes her coffee and peach pie. The coffee was strong. She would most likely be awake for some of the night as a result. She leaves the payment along with a good tip, takes her paperback back to her bag and then leaves. The young woman from the couple earlier takes a notice of her appearance.

"How was the café?" asks the receptionist woman as Veronica gets back to the motel.

"Nice. It was nice." She says.

"Well, I'm glad to recommend it."

"Do you mind if I ask if there are other guests here now?"

"Yeah. There is a family consisting of a dad and his son.

There's also a guy who booked a room this evening. Why do you ask?"

"Just wondering."

She returns to her room. enables the lights. opens a beer can and begins to consume. She wants to play music through a speaker, but the atmosphere in the motel isn't appropriate. They might hear if there were any other people on the floor. She decides against doing that and instead wears her headphones to listen to music while sipping her beer.

The next morning, when she woke up, it was already 11 a.m. on the clock. She gets up and thinks for a while, sitting on her bed, whether to pass the day here and then start tomorrow or whether she should leave right now. The quiet atmosphere is something she adores more than anything. So staying here by herself for a day doesn't sound like a bad option to her. She eventually decides to stay for the day. She gets up from her bed to freshen herself up. She looks at herself in the mirror for a while. Her hair looks messy. She takes off her clothes and walks towards the shower. She takes a cold shower while singing. She keeps her voice down as much as possible as she sings.

After her shower, she dresses in dark denim shorts and an oversized t-shirt. Packing a few necessaries in her bag and leaving the rest on her bed, she ties her Converse laces, locks her door, and then descends the stairs to reach the reception area. This time, the woman from last night wasn't present at the reception. Instead, a young woman, around 25 years old, was sitting there, engrossed in a slim magazine. Her neck appears to be covered in tattoos. She looks professional because of the way she was dressed, with a formal shirt neatly tucked into her skirt. She is wearing a golden-colored watch.

"Excuse me, where's the woman who was here last night?" Veronica asks.

"Her shift starts after 7 p.m. Until then, it's my shift. If you require any assistance, I can help you," the young woman replies in a formal tone.

"I see. I was about to head to the woods up front, near the main road. Do you know if it's safe out there or not?"

"It's okay as long as you don't go too deep. The area is too remote to get a search team on time if you get lost. So keep your tracks and make sure to return before it gets too dark. That should be fine, in my opinion."

"Alright. Thanks for letting me know. Can you keep the keys for me?"

"Yeah, sure. Have a good day."

"Thanks, you too."

As she drives along the main road, Veronica notices the

man from last night, one of the young couple at the café, sitting under a tree, smoking. Her car passes by him, but he doesn't seem to pay any attention to it. Veronica takes a right turn into the forest through a narrow path, but it's enough for her car to pass through. She drives about a kilometer deep into the woods and then decides to stop. Turning off the engine, she steps out of the car. The sky is a bit overcast, but the air feels fresh. Taking in a deep breath, she allows the fresh air to fill her lungs, exhaling with contentment. She scans her eyes around the surroundings for a while, taking in the peaceful ambiance. The birds' chirping is the only sound breaking the silence. Here, there's no artificial noise, only the sounds of nature. All of a sudden, she remembers what the strange man told her yesterday. After removing her bag from the backseat, Veronica carefully opens her diary. She reads what she had written down yesterday as she flips through the pages. She gives the diary a quick once-over before putting it back in her bag. She settles into a tidy and comfortable spot beneath a nearby tree. When she finishes eating, she pulls out a cigarette from the pack, lights it up, and takes a drag, exhaling a plume of smoke into the air. Veronica gets up, puts on her headphones, and starts listening to music while walking back and forth in the same spot. The sky quickly darkens, and raindrops begin to fall. Before she knows it, the rain starts pouring heavily. She hurries back to where her bag is kept, grabs it, and rushes to the car. Sitting inside, she locks the door as the rain continues to pour outside. She comes to the conclusion that getting wet in the rain is no longer wrong. She considers it for a moment before deciding to enjoy the rain because she has no obligations and no one to warn her about getting sick. She extends her arms as she exits the vehicle into the downpour, allowing the raindrops to cover her entire body. Although the cold rain makes her skin tremble, she keeps her eyes closed and her face tipped upward because she is mesmerised by the scene. She imagines that if her life were a movie, a happy soundtrack would be playing in the background right now as she stands in the rain, feeling the water soak her skin and clothes. She smiles at the thought as she continues to take in the rain, feeling liberated and content in that serene moment.

As Veronica drives back to the motel, memories of her grandma flood her mind. She recalls how her grandma used to sing Joni Mitchell's 'Both Sides Now' on special occasions, especially on Veronica's birthdays. It was a beautiful song, but Veronica never fully understood it the way her grandma did. Her grandma's rendition of the song was enchanting, as if Joni Mitchell's spirit had possessed her, and she sang each note with perfection. However, on Veronica's 18th birthday, her grandma was no longer there to sing the song, and that memory always lingered in her heart. She fondly remembered a rainy day from her childhood when she was sitting with her grandma on the porch of their house. The rain was pouring heavily, creating a beautiful scene outside. Curious about the experience of being in the rain, nine-year-old Veronica asked her grandma how it felt.

Her grandma replied, "Haven't you ever tried it yourself?"

"No," Veronica replied. She hasn't experimented with as much on her own. She was likely indoors reading a book of tales while the neighbourhood kids her age were outside having fun and running around. But that doesn't prove that she wasn't enjoying herself. She prefers doing that to playing with other kids.

"Then let me show you how it feels to be in the rain," her grandma said with a smile. She stood up, walked out of the porch, and started to get drenched in the rainfall.

"Come on, feel it yourself," her grandma urged, extending her arms towards Veronica.

"But Mom says I'll catch a cold if I get wet in the rain," Veronica hesitated.

Her grandma replied, "Sometimes, my dear, you have to do things you're not supposed to in order to enjoy life.

Sometimes happiness lies in breaking the rules."

Veronica brings her car to a halt as the memories of her grandma's wise words flood her mind. Retrieving her bag from the back seat, she takes out her diary and pens down the unforgettable advice her grandma shared that rainy day: *"Sometimes, you have to do things you're not supposed to in order to enjoy life. Sometimes happiness lies in breaking the rules."*

Veronica arrives back at the motel in the afternoon. The woman at the reception glances at her and comments, "You should have taken a raincoat with you."

"No, it's alright. I did it intentionally," Veronica replies.

"Alright then, hope you had fun."

"Yeah, definitely. Have you ever been in the rain?" Veronica asks.

"Me? Yeah, I think once I was heading home from work and it started to rain heavily. Before I found a place to hide, I was soaking wet."

"How did it feel?"

"Feel? I don't know, just usual. But it would have been better if I found a shelter before getting wet," she replies.

"Alright."

Veronica has a part of her that believes the woman probably doesn't have any fun in her. She has never experienced being drenched in rain. However, another part of her believes that since she is living her life to her preferences, that is how it ought to be. Not everybody has the same priorities. Everybody is unique, and they all have different desires. For instance, she was regarded as boring by the majority of her classmates. But she was acting appropriately. She was engaging in behaviour that she found enjoyable.

Veronica takes her keys from the receptionist and heads up the stairs to her room. Upon entering, she throws her bag on the bed and then goes to the bathroom mirror. Her T-shirt is already drying, but her hair is still wet. As she looks at herself in the mirror, she feels good about it. It's a new and strange feeling for her, one she has never experienced before. She touches her hair, raising her left hand and shaking it. She makes different facial expressions, observing herself closely. In the end, she smiles, thinking she's probably doing something silly. She takes off her wet clothes and changes into dry ones. Taking out a can of food and a beer, she sits on the bed facing towards the window and starts eating. The rain has stopped, and the clouds have cleared, leaving a purple hue on the horizon. She remembers another quote from Dead Poets Society, *"Seize the day. Make your lives extraordinary."* No wonder today she had done just that. A gentle smile appears on her face as she thinks about her day and the freedom she felt.

Veronica decides to have dinner at the same place she went yesterday. She drives to the café, and this time, it's more crowded than before. Most of the seats are filled, but she spots an empty one. 'A Foggy Day' by Oscar Peterson plays on the speaker. The young couple from yesterday is also there, sitting on the last row of the left corner where the old man was sitting before. She takes the same seat as yesterday, since it's still available.

The same waitress from yesterday approaches her with a smile and says, "Good evening, may I take your order?"

"Yes, a black coffee and peach pie, please." Veronica replies, just like she did yesterday, even though it's not usual for someone to order only peach pie for dinner. She likes to keep her meal light.

As the waitress goes away she brings out the same paperback she read yesterday sitting here. She opens the page where the bookmark was kept and starts reading from where she left off. Even though the place is more noisy than yesterday, it doesn't bother her to focus. She always had an extraordinary ability to focus. Nothing distracts her when she's absorbed in something. After reading a few pages, the waitress arrives with her order. She thanks the waitress and keeps her paperback aside, pulling the coffee cup closer to her right hand. Then she lights up a cigarette, takes up her paperback, and continues reading. The music changes to 'Blue in Green' by Miles Davis.

Almost two hours have passed as she reads her book in the café. The waitress has refilled her coffee several times, and she has smoked five cigarettes. The ashtray is filled with cigarette butts. The plate of peach pie is empty now. The café has become less crowded, with only five customers remaining, including her. Two women sit in front of the next row, gossiping quietly with their drinks. A guy engages in a small conversation with the attendant, who sits close to her. Another guy sits next to the two women, scrolling through his phone. She closes her book as she finishes reading, puts it back in her bag, leaves the bill along with a generous tip on the table, and then gets up. The guy sitting behind her takes a glance at her as she walks towards the exit. She looks back at the café before getting into her car. She would have taken a photo if she had brought her camera with her, but she left it in her motel room.

Heading back to her motel room, she tries to fall asleep, but something seems to keep her awake. It's not the first time that she his having hard time falling asleep. She frequently struggled to get to sleep at night. Particularly recently, she has experienced extreme daytime sleepiness when she is at home. She doesn't sleep though. She either watches films or reads. She believes that taking a nap in the middle of the day is not a good idea. She also performs the same actions at night when she has trouble sleeping. But one day, she fell asleep while watching a film. The film was at the 35th minute when she paused it and fell asleep. She woke up about an hour later. Then she starts to see the film again. A strange observation comes to her mind as she does that. She felt like, even though she had taken a long break in between, when she started watching the film, it felt to her as if nothing had happened. The one hour that she spent sleeping is hollow. Watching the film from where she left off now feels like there hasn't been a break in between at all.

At one point, she finds it almost impossible to fall asleep at that time, so she gets up. Checking the time on her phone, it's 1:37 a.m. She tucks her knees into her chest with her head leaning against them, thinking for a while about what to do. Eventually, she gets up and starts packing her bag. She decides to leave and head towards her destination. She takes a black button-down shirt and white gabardine pants from her bag and dresses herself with them. Veronica stands in front of the bathroom mirror and brushes her hair carefully, ensuring she looks presentable. Satisfied that she's ready to go, she double-checks the room to make sure she hasn't left anything behind. Taking her bag on her shoulder, she turns off the light, locks the door, and heads towards the reception area. This time, the older woman from last night is back at the reception. Veronica notices her engaged in a quiet conversation on the telephone, so she places her bag on the couch and patiently waits for a moment. Once the receptionist finishes her call, Veronica pays for the room. The woman appears somewhat surprised by her decision to leave at such a late hour.

"You sure you wanna leave now?" the receptionist asks.

"Yeah, why?" Veronica responds.

"I don't know. It's pitch black outside, and it's a peculiar hour to leave, especially when you're in a place like this. And most people come to this motel just to spend the night and leave once the sun comes up, you know what I'm saying."

"Well, yeah, I was trying to fall asleep but failed, so I decided to leave. I'll be in my car driving anyway, so I think it's gonna be okay."

"I hope so. Where are you headed to anyway?"

"The Ozarks."

"I see. Enjoy your trip."

"Do you mind if I ask you something?" Veronica's voice

is curious.

"No, sure, ask."

"How long have you been working here?"

"Nine months. Why?"

"Just curious. Has there ever been a night when there's no guest and you're just by yourself in the whole motel?"

"Yeah, it's happened several times."

"Don't you feel creepy?"

"I try not to think about it," the receptionist replies with a hint of unease.

"Okay. I understand. Anyway, thanks for the room," she says as she starts walking towards the exist.

"You're always welcome."

As she's leaving, she stops for a moment, as if remembering something. She gets back to her and asks, "One more question, is there any guest currently in room 209?"

"No. That room is not booked." She replies.

"Was there anyone yesterday night?"

"No. That room hasn't been booked in a while. I can assure you that. Why?"

"Oh, nothing. Just wondering." She says it with a smile and leaves.

The woman thinks for a while about what she has just said, trying to figure something out of it.

When Veronica reaches the parking space, she notices that there are only two cars this time, including hers. She gets into her car and starts the engine, but she can't help but think about it for a while. If one of the cars belongs to the father and son, then there are only three people in the motel now. If it's the car of the guy who's staying alone, then there are only two people. It feels a bit eerie to her in an area like this. What's even stranger is that she has been here for more than a day and she hasn't come across any of the other guests.

As Veronica continues driving, the road stretches ahead, flanked by dense woods on either side. The moonlight filters through the leaves, casting eerie shadows on the ground. The air is still and cool, carrying the scent of wet earth after the recent rain. The sound of crickets fills the silence. The road seems endless, winding through the darkness, and the occasional hooting of an owl adds to the mysterious atmosphere. But that doesn't reach her ears, as her window is locked this time. No music is playing either. Her car is the only moving presence on the road, and the headlights cut through the darkness, illuminating the path ahead as she travels through the night. After an hour or so, the darkness of the night gradually gives way to the first signs of dawn. The horizon starts to glow with a soft, golden hue as the sun prepares to rise. The distant stars begin to fade, and the sky transitions from a deep midnight blue to a lighter shade, tinged with pink and orange. The landscape around her becomes more visible as the sun's rays slowly illuminate the world. Trees and hills take shape in the growing light, and the road ahead becomes clearer. The night's silence starts to give way to the awakening sounds of nature - the chirping of birds, the rustling of leaves, and the distant calls of animals. As the morning breeze blows through the open window, Veronica inhales deeply. The earth is awakening from its sleep, and the air smells like dewy grass and is crisp and refreshing. Compared to yesterday's aroma in the forest, this one is different. Her senses appear to be refreshed by the morning breeze, which also gives her a sense of calmness. She can't help but smile as the wind tousles her hair, accepting the mess as a symbol of freedom.

When morning comes, She decides to look for a place to eat breakfast because she is feeling hungry. She enters a quaint café she sees along the road. She takes a seat by the window and is greeted by an inviting smell of coffee and freshly baked goods. She strolls into the café and orders a cup of coffee, toast, and scrambled eggs. The café isn't very crowded. Veronica looks out through the glass window and observes the quiet street scene. A man walks by with his dog, and a young woman strolls while engrossed in her cellphone.

The waiter brings her breakfast, and Veronica begins to eat. She starts with the toast, then moves on to the scrambled eggs, and finally washes it all down with a steaming cup of coffee. Three young girls, probably around fifteen or sixteen years old, enter the café with their schoolbags on their backs. Veronica glances at them briefly. After finishing her coffee, she sits for a moment, lost in thought. Then, she leaves the bill without leaving a tip this time and gets to her car. Opening the door, she sits in the driver's seat. Her eyes feel heavy, and tiredness overcomes her. Deciding to take a short nap, she turns her body to the right, pulls her legs up onto the seat, and closes her eyes. The soft morning light filters through the window, gently touching her face as she falls into a deep sleep.

CHAPTER THREE

Where is Your Blue Hat?

She wakes up around 11 am. She realizes she had a peaceful sleep. It's been a long time since she felt this rested. However, before waking up, she had a strange dream. In the dream, she found herself back in the motel room, but this time her family was there with her. Her brother Kevin mentioned that he was going out, but her father objected. Veronica sat on the bed, facing the window, and listened to the interactions of her family members. The dream seemed utterly nonsensical to her, leaving her puzzled about its meaning. All of our dreams, according to her grandmother, contain some sort of meaning. Whether or not we comprehend it will depend on that. But none of us can really comprehend the significance of any dream. A dream may be positive and make us feel better when we wake up from it, but it can also have negative connotations. On the other hand, a nightmare occasionally has a useful purpose in life. It wasn't a pleasant dream, but it also wasn't a bad one. What significance this might have, she wonders.

She continues her journey on the highway, maintaining a steady speed. The scenic view outside the car window captivates her as the landscapes change gradually. The road stretches ahead, and her focus remains on the path ahead. With one hand on the wheel, she occasionally takes a drag from the cigarette between her lips, its smoke intertwining with the fresh breeze that flows through the open window. The road is her companion, and the world outside her car is an ever-changing canvas of natural beauty. Her playlist shuffles, and 'Both Sides Now' by Joni Mitchell begins to play. And as soon as that occurs, she begins to remember her grandma more frequently. When Veronica was fifteen years old, grandma once explained to her how crucial it is for a woman to select a good man for her life. She warned that she will meet a lot of men as she gets older, and most of them will be lying when they tell her that she's special and stuff. She said she should know, obviously, that she's so special, but she doesn't need them to tell her that she is. Veronica recognised the advice her grandmother gave, knowing she shouldn't let other people's viewpoints control her life. She understood that letting outside factors influence her choices might have unanticipated results. She did, however, conceal something that day: her true feelings regarding her own preferences. She had never admitted to her grandmother that she was attracted to girls and wasn't interested in boys. She had kept this aspect of herself hidden out of concern for her family's reaction or comprehension. This secret weighs heavily on her as she continues to drive. While she is grateful for the lessons her grandmother taught her, she also wishes she had the courage to be truly herself around the people she cares about the most. As Joni Mitchell's voice accompanies her on her journey, she thinks about the complexity of her feelings.

Veronica maintains a steady pace. The landscape changes, and the hours pass by. She glances at the odometer, calculating the remaining distance. As she takes another drag from her cigarette, she reflects on the fact that she has smoked four packets since starting her journey. It's more than she usually smokes on regular days. Smoking has become a coping mechanism, helping her ease her mind and stay focused on the road ahead. She occasionally opens the window to let fresh air in, balancing the smoke-filled car with the cool breeze. Her mind drifts back to the time when she started smoking. It was when she was sixteen. She was sitting in the backyard of her school while reading in her after-school hours, and the school was almost empty. Most of those who stayed for club work were also gone. But she was still there, absorbed deep in her reading. All of a sudden, she sees Catherine walking towards her with a smile. Catherine was the closest to her among her classmates. She wasn't that close to anyone, but if she ever had to talk about something, she talked with Catherine. And Catherine did the same with her. Even though Catherine had other circles of friends, she always relied on Veronica for any advice, as she thought Veronica might be the wisest person to talk to about anything. Catherine sat beside her and said, "What's up?"

"Nothing, just usual. "How about you?"

"Cool. Do you smoke?" she asked while lighting up a cigarette.

"No."

"You wanna try?"

"Well, I guess I will." She replied, and Catherine handed over the cigarette to her. She had never specifically considered starting to smoke. That didn't pique her interest. She saw it as a self-destructive choice even though other girls her age tended to think it was cool. She reasoned that something that consumes a person from the inside out cannot be cool. However, after Catherine had inquired, she made the decision to try.

She took a drag from it and started coughing. And immediately regretted doing so.

"Well, it's normal for it to happen the first time." Said Catherine.

She took another drag, and this time she was at ease. But she didn't feel anything special about it.

"Do you smoke often?"

"Yeah, these days I smoke a lot. That day at Cynthia's place, we smoked a huge joint too. Man, it was wild." Catherine replied with a cheerful tone.

"Were you guys stoned?"

"Mostly. Jenny started talking about some French guy inventing weed and that he secretly tends to take over the world with it, which didn't make any sense, but at that time we were paying so much attention to whatever she was saying. You should join us sometimes." Catherine explained, laughing.

"I'll see about that." Said Veronica.

A few days later, after that, she started yearning for a smoke as she was reading René Descartes on a park bench. She went to the store nearby and bought a pack of camels, and she smoked two of them while reading. That is where it all started. Since then, she has forgotten when the last time she smoked less than ten cigarettes a day. It's always more than ten. The habit seems to have taken hold of her, becoming an inseparable part of her routine. She thinks about it sometimes too, realising the toll it might be taking on her health and well-being. Yet, she is determined to quit smoking as soon as she turns twenty. This is what she tells herself every time the thought of smoking too much crosses her mind. It's one of her goal and she hopes to make it a reality when the time comes. She doesn't consciously think it's possible though. There is no turning back once someone has held those thin sticks between their fingertips and touched them with their lips, breathed in their intoxicating essence into their lungs, and then exhaled it into the open air. The act develops into more than just a habit; it creates a connection and an emotional bond stronger than a promise of marriage between two lovers. The idea of giving up cigarettes makes her feel as though she is saying goodbye to a piece of herself, and the thought of breaking this bond seems almost unfathomable. She is determined to stop smoking, but she can't help but feel that cigarettes have become too ingrained in her life.

As her memories take her back to her high school days, she recalls another person from her past – Simon. He was also a quiet type, just like her. Rarely did he engage in conversations with others. One day, when Catherine was absent, She found herself having lunch alone. Unexpectedly, Simon approached her table and asked if he could sit there. She gave him the go-ahead, and they both ate their meals in silence. Strangely enough, she wasn't bothered by the lack of conversation. She couldn't tell what he felt or if he was nervous, but he didn't seem that way.

On another day when Catherine was absent again, Simon once again approached her, seeking permission to sit across from her. After a few minutes of quiet, he asked, "Do you play any instrument?"

"I play the piano sometimes. Why?" Veronica responded. She couldn't help but wonder if he was attempting to start a conversation or if the question just popped into his head while they were eating. Either way, he was weird. But that didn't bother her much because she considered herself a little peculiar too. In her opinion, everyone had their quirks, whether they acknowledged it or not.

"Just curious. I play the saxophone," he casually replied.

"Okay," Veronica said.

He asked, seemingly hoping for a surprised response, "Have you ever met anyone who plays the saxophone?"

She shook her head, her interest dim. "No," she said.

He nudged her, "Don't you want to know why I'm interested in the saxophone?"

"Why?" Despite having a small amount of curiosity, Veronica asked.

"Well, it's because I think it's a unique instrument, not something just anyone can play. But I didn't learn to play it for the sake of uniqueness. I've been fascinated by it since I started listening to music. My dad was a huge jazz fan, and our house was always filled with jazz records. I used to listen to them all the time. Sonny Rollins is my favourite saxophone player. I was truly captivated by his solos, and I think I took up the saxophone just because of him," He explained as if he has been heard for the first time.

"That's nice." Veronica said. She almost felt pity for him. This is the first time she has seen him be expressive or talk about something with interest. A side of him that probably nobody sees at all. That's the way of life. Two types of people don't talk much. The ones who have nothing to say and the other ones are those who have so much to say. She assumed he was the second type.

He fell quiet once more, seeming to realize his attempt to talk didn't go as planned. Veronica felt a sort of regret in the air, as if he wished he hadn't said so much. They just sat there eating without speaking. A small feeling of sympathy for him started to grow inside her. She understood he might have tried to open up, but it didn't quite work out. While she wanted to say something, another part of her hesitated, caught between reaching out and staying in their usual quiet zone. She felt some sort of guilt because of that, even though there was nothing to be considered her fault.

After that day, he never approached her, even when there was an empty seat next to her. They never spoke again. It felt as if that interaction had never occurred, just like two strangers briefly locking eyes while passing the street, but once they've moved on, neither looks back. The shared moment remains confined to those fleeting seconds of eye contact. Although she hadn't been particularly interested in him, a tinge of regret always accompanied her thoughts about what transpired.

As she drives, memories continue to surface in her mind. She reflects on the brevity of life and the futility of holding onto regrets. She realizes that making choices, even if uncertain, is often better than dwelling in hesitation.

The afternoon sun begins to wane, creating gentle hues across the horizon. Veronica finds herself not far from her intended destination, according to the map. The surroundings have transformed into a soothing expanse of deep green forests on either side of the road. This shift in scenery brings her a renewed sense of contentment. The lush landscapes continue to unfold before her. The soft caress of the evening breeze through the open window adds a delightful fragrance to the experience, soothing her spirit further.

The sun sinks lower, making long shadows. Her attention is drawn to a figure on the side of the road. A young girl stands there, her arms waving in a hopeful gesture, seeking a ride. Drawing nearer, Veronica observes the girl's attire: a neatly buttoned shirt, stylishly tucked into skinny jeans, and a backpack resting comfortably on her shoulders. She slows down when she gets closer and turns off the music. She hits the break and nods her head, allowing the girl to get in. The girl thanks her with a smile, sits beside her, and locks the door. Her blonde hair is shortly cut to her neck. Anyone who looks at her will immediately notice how symmetrical her face appears to be. She was stunningly beautiful. the kind of attractive that, if she were to ride in a lift with a bunch of people, she would draw everyone's attention.

"Where are you heading?" she asks.

"I don't know yet. I just got here." Veronica replies.

"Well, I guess you're in luck." She takes a pause and looks

at Veronica with a smile, then looks away and continues, "You can go to the Blue Lane or whispering pines. Both are pretty good if you are willing to stay here for a few days. Blue Lane will give you a view of the lake, while Whispering Pines has more green-filled architecture. I would prefer Blue Lane, though. Also, I live near Blue Lane." she says in an enthusiastic voice.

"Sounds good enough."

"I'm Olivia by the way."

"You can call me Veronica."

"*Veronica, Veronica, jouw liefste zei vaarwel, Maar 's avonds in het donker dan komen tranen snel.*" She sings with a melody. "Do you know the song?"

"No. What language is this?"

"Sweadish. It's titled 'Veronica' by Cornelis Vreeswijk." She again looks at Veronica with a smile and then sings again, "*Veronica, Veronica, waar is je blauwe hoed? Je liefste is gaan zoeken, maar zoekt jouw lief wel goed? Jouw liefste is verdwenen, misschien zie je hem weer, in de morgen.*"

"What does that mean?" Veronica asks with curiosity.

"It says, Veronica, Veronica, where is your blue hat? Your beloved is going to seek, but is your search for your love working? Your beloved is gone, maybe you'll see him again in the morning."

"How do you know Swedish?"

"I speak three languages. English, Japanese, and Swedish."

"How did you learn the other two?"

"Well, my mother was from Sweden. So I didn't have to learn it with effort. It was more like a mother tongue. I grew up with her."

"Your mother was?"

Yeah, she passed away two years ago." Olivia replies, looking through the window on her side.

Veronica takes a glance at her and says, "Sorry about that."

"It's alright. Nothing to be sorry for."

"And how did you learn Japanese?"

"I'm majoring in Japanese Literature," Olivia shares with a thoughtful smile. "Back in middle school, I used to read Japanese literature, but of course, it was in translation. Still, they fascinated me. There's something about Japanese literature that has a unique pull. So, I decided to read them in their original language. I learned Japanese and applied for Japanese literature in college," she explains.

"That's really cool." Veronica speaks while keeping her focus on the road. Now that the sun has completely set, the only lights guiding them are the headlights of the cars.

"Do you like literature?" Olivia asks.

"Yeah. I love reading literature but I don't study them like you do. I don't know much Japanese writers except Haruki Murakami and Yoko Tawada."

"Who's your favourite writer?"

"That is actually a difficult question to answer." Veronica replies.

"Then you must read a lot. That's why you have too many to pick from."

Veronica nods with a faint smile "I think so."

"Take the right turn next, and then go left at the end of the road," Olivia instructs, her hands indicating the directions.

Veronica follows her guidance while asking, "Are the streets always this quiet after dark?"

"Mostly. There's actually not much to see at night around here, except for the bars, cafes, and casinos."

Veronica realizes, "Wait, we're already at the motel. Where should I drop you?"

Olivia's mischievous smile appears as she replies, "Don't worry. I'll walk from here. But first, I'll help you book a room. I know people around."

They get out of the car after parking in an appropriate place. Veronica gets her heavy bag from the backseat. The motel's exterior is a striking illustration of minimalist architecture. Its two-story design emphasises clear lines and practical aesthetics. The walls, which are particularly thick, give off a strong impression. The building's form is a tasteful blend of modern simplicity, with a neutral colour scheme that blends in with the surroundings.

They step into the expansive ground-floor area. Veronica's gaze falls upon the reception area situated to the left. A young boy, likely around sixteen or seventeen, stands behind the counter, engrossed in scrolling through his phone. Olivia addresses him by name, and he looks up.

"Hey Finn!"

"Hey there! Where have you been this afternoon?" Finn's tone carries the casual warmth of someone accustomed to Olivia's presence.

"Just wandered around for a bit. Anyway, this is Veronica. She'll be staying here for a while, so find her a good room."

Veronica offers a friendly greeting, "Hi!"

"Hi, I'm Finn. Nice to meet you," he replies. "Let's see what room I can sort out for you. Single bed, right?"

"Yes, please."

"Alright. Follow me," Finn invites, leading them away from the reception area and down the hallway.

As they begin to walk, Olivia turns to Veronica and says, "Well, I'll be on my way. Come by the lake tomorrow morning. You'll find me there. Thanks for the ride. See you around."

"Thanks to you too for the motel. I'll catch you tomorrow then," Veronica responds, her steps matching Finn's pace as they proceed down the corridor.

They go up the stairs to the second floor, and Finn takes her to the last room on the left, marked as Room 211. He unlocks the door, switches on the lights, and then shows her around. The room is bigger than what she had before.

As you enter, the bed is on the right side, and it's larger than a typical single bed, almost enough for two people. Straight ahead is the bathroom, and it's easy to find. On the other side of the room, there's a glass-enclosed balcony with a chair and table. Across from the entrance, a big TV hangs on the wall, right in the center. The bed is by the window, and there's a table next to it with a small lamp for reading or working. The room looks really comfy and well-equipped.

Veronica throws her bag casually onto the bed after Finn leaves and neatly arranges her books and diary on the table. She sips a beer and munches on a can of food after a brief refreshment. She takes a seat at the table and grabs a pen and her diary. She is seated at the table with her head resting against her right hand and a pen in her left hand resting above the open pages of her diary. Her mind plays back memories of her most recent encounter with Olivia like a movie. Olivia's animated speech and her capacity to conjure up a magical atmosphere around her drew everything in the universe in. Her symmetrical face and contagious smile remain in Veronica's mind. She summarises the encounter and records every detail in her diary to show how she got to this point. Later, she stands up, opens the glass door, and steps onto the balcony. Although the surroundings are mostly in darkness, she can still appreciate the tranquil sight. The wide expanse of the lake is visible from here. She puts on her headphones that were hanging around her neck, connects them to her phone, and starts shuffling her playlist. The song 'Anchor' by Novo Amor starts playing.

When she wakes up the following morning, it has already passed seven. Dim sunlight enters the space through the curtains that are only partially drawn. She gets up, stretches, and goes to the balcony. She is in awe of the scene in front of her, which is a landscape painted in greens and blues. The chilly morning breeze refreshes her mind as the colours meld and dance. She changes into casual clothes and dons a blue baseball hat before heading downstairs. Finn is still at the reception, busy with his phone.

"Hi there!" Veronica greets.

"Hey! What can I do for you?" Finn asks, setting his phone down.

"I'm wondering where I can grab breakfast around here."

"Absolutely. Just head down this corridor and turn right. You'll find the back door of the motel. There's a café right in front, by the lakeside. You can enjoy your breakfast with a stunning view." Finn informs.

"Alright then, great, thank you."

"My pleasure." Finn says with a smile.

She heads in the direction Finn pointed, and indeed, the sight before her is as impressive as he had described. The café is a cozy spot with a simple setup – a shaded area with a counter for orders, and tables and chairs nestled beneath the protective canopy. Several individuals are already seated there, most likely guests from the motel. Others have even moored their boats nearby, taking a moment to enjoy a cup of coffee along the lakeside. Veronica's surprise grows as she spots Olivia behind the café counter, taking orders and interacting with customers. With a warm smile, she greets Olivia and engages in conversation.

"Hey!" Veronica says.

Olivia raises her head, pleasantly surprised by Veronica's presence. "Oh, hey! Good morning."

"Morning. I had no idea you worked here."

"Well, now you do. What can I get you? It's on the house."

"That's really nice of you. Thanks. I'll just go with a black coffee."

"Sure thing, just coffee? Nothing else?"

"No, thanks."

"Alright then, your black coffee will be ready in a moment."

Olivia hands her the coffee. Veronica thanks her and walks her way to take a seat as Olivia rises her voice and says, "Hey, I'll be out in an hour. So, maybe if you wanna have a walk together later?"

"Sure. That would be great." She says looking back.

Her focus briefly shifts to Olivia as she sits by the lake, enjoying her coffee and the picturesque surroundings. Her thoughts are caught up in the mysterious appeal of Olivia. She finds herself debating whether Her presence or the natural beauty surrounding her is more captivating. She knows that long stares might come off as odd, so she controls herself from staring at Olivia for too long. She is aware of her apparent magnetic pull on her, a pull that could easily keep her gaze averted without a second thought.

Veronica spots Olivia approaching with a brisk pace, meeting her by the motel's exterior wall where Veronica had been waiting. Olivia's attire exudes a comfortable style — a snug cotton sweater paired with denim shorts and classic black Vans sneakers.

"Sorry for the wait," Olivia apologizes.

"No worries," Veronica replies, and they set off in the same direction.

Olivia's attention turns to Veronica's blue baseball hat. "Nice hat, by the way," she remarks. "It's blue, too, just like that song I mentioned yesterday."

"Seems like it is." Veronica responds, stealing a quick glance at Olivia. "It's kinda cold around here," she adds.

"It does get chilly during this time. Don't tell me you didn't pack any warm clothes," Olivia teases.

Veronica chuckles. "Actually, I didn't. I wasn't aware it would be this cold."

Olivia raises an eyebrow playfully. "So, you're not exactly a tourist, huh? You come during the off-season, and now you're telling me you didn't bring any warm clothes? Did you run away from home?"

They both share a laugh before Veronica answers, "Well, actually, this is my first time traveling alone. I just felt like getting away, you know? To have an experience, something like that. And for some reason, I felt drawn to come here. So, I followed my instinct."

Olivia smiles. "That's interesting. There might be a reason your instincts guided you here."

"Like what?" Veronica asks.

"Something like precognition. Have you ever read any books by Lucy Stanfield?"

"No, I've never heard of her," Veronica admits.

Olivia explains, "She's a local writer. In one of her books, she described how our past and future exist simultaneously. We can't see it, but we can sometimes feel it. For example, if you suddenly feel a strong urge to become a musician, that means a reality where you're a musician already exists in the future. It's like a potential path. Now, it's up to your choices. If you take the steps and follow that path, you'll see that reality come true. If you don't, you'll experience a different path. So, if you felt drawn to come here, it's probably because your subconscious mind knows there's something here for you."

Veronica listens attentively, mulling over her words. "That's actually pretty interesting. I never thought of it that way."

Olivia chuckles softly. "Well, the entire universe is fascinating. There's so much we don't know. We only know what's already been uncovered. But there's a vast expanse of undiscovered things out there. In a way, we're still in the realm of knowing nothing."

"So, you believe in spirituality?" Veronica asks.

Olivia thoughtfully answers, "Well, it doesn't really matter what I personally believe in. The truth is already out there, and what I do know is that there must be some kind of divine force capable of making anything possible. Every belief system is grounded in that idea. The only error people tend to make is assuming that their own belief is the absolute truth, when that might not necessarily be the case."

They move along the streets in peace and quiet. They are shielded from the sun by the overhanging trees. Conversation is occasionally infused with a crisp breeze that occasionally brushes against their skin. A purple Mercedes hums steadily past them in this serene setting.

"Anyway, Lucy Stanfield is attending a press event at my university tomorrow for her new book release," Olivia says. "Would you be interested in going there with me?"

"Yeah, sure. I'd be glad to."

"And come to my place. I'll lend you some warm clothes. I think mine will fit you perfectly."

Veronica gives a nervous smile. "You sure that's okay?"

"Totally."

CHAPTER FOUR

On Board

Olivia's room resembles a library. A sizable bookshelf stands prominently in front of them. The walls are painted a soothing light blue. A small wall clock adorns the left side of the room. A portrait of a lady graces one wall, its origins unfamiliar to Veronica. A table hosts an array of more books, their pages yellowed by the passage of time. A window offers a direct view of the verdant woods, though she assumes it might feel a bit eerie at night.

"Are these all yours?" Veronica inquires, gesturing towards the books on the shelves.

"No. My mom's books are here too, all together," Olivia responds.

"She was a reader too?"

"She was a professor at the university I attend now."

"That's cool."

72

Olivia comes up with a hoodie and a nice cotton sweater. "Try these," she says.

Veronica puts the hoodie on and studies herself in the mirror. It fits her perfectly. The color is blue with a round logo printed on it which is unfamiliar to her. She leans closer to the mirror, examining herself closely.

"See? That fits you perfectly," Olivia remarks while observing her.

"I guess so."

"So, what are your plans for the day?"

"I don't know. I haven't decided anything."

"I kinda figured you would say something like that," Olivia says with a soft chuckle.

"You wanna roam around the lake on a boat?"

"I'm kinda scared of deep water. I don't know how to swim."

"No way, you don't know how to swim?"

"No."

"It's alright, it's not like you're gonna get drowned. Come on. It's gonna be fun, don't worry." Olivia says as she grabs her hand, leading her towards the exit. The touch of her hand feels to her as if she has awakened from a deep sleep. It reminds her of how touch-deprived she has been lately, and this is probably the first time in a long while that she has felt a human touch. And sometimes a simple thing like a touch can mean a lot to someone. And that is exactly what she felt at that moment.

"What if I drown?" She asks.

"I will save you."

A small boardwalk has a few boats and jet skis gently moored along it. Sunlight reflects the clear sky above as it dances on the water's surface. The surroundings are given a sense of tranquilly by the stillness in the air, which adds to the atmosphere's peacefulness. A middle-aged man appears busy in repairing a boat, his attention consumed by the task at hand. Unperturbed by the approaching girls, he remains focused on his work. Olivia breaks the silence, calling out, "Hey Jerry!"

Startled, the man looks up and greets them, "Hey, what's up?"

Olivia introduces Veronica, "Meet my friend Veronica. She's from Columbus." Jerry raises a friendly hand in greeting, reciprocated by her wave.

Olivia explains their plan, "I was wondering if I could borrow one of your boats to show her around."

"Sure thing. Just remember not to take too long. The afternoons get pretty busy, and I might run short on boats.

Keep that in mind," Jerry advises.

"Don't worry, we'll be mindful of that," Olivia assures.

"Take the one in the right corner." he directs.

Olivia jumps onto the boat and extends a hand to help Veronica on board.

"You seem to know almost everyone here," she remarks as Olivia starts the boat's engine.

She chuckles softly, her eyes focused ahead. "Well, I grew up here. So, yeah, I know almost everyone. Jerry, for instance, was a friend of my dad's."

Veronica hesitates briefly, then decides to ask about her dad, "What about your dad? What does he do?"

"He's in Italy. My parents got divorced when I was thirteen."

"I'm sorry to hear that."

Olivia's response is reassuring, "It's alright, don't be."

The boat glides smoothly over the water, the serene lake landscape captivates Veronica's attention. Despite the absence of wind, the boat's motion generates a breeze, causing the strands of hair outside her hat to dance playfully. The boat's speed makes her slightly uneasy, and she clings tightly to her seat. She raises her voice to be heard above the engine's noise, addressing Olivia.

"I'm kinda scared,"

Olivia chuckles warmly, "Do you know the song that goes like, *'So you should get on board, with someone whose course is steadier than mine'*?"

"No," she replies.

"It's called 'On Board' by Alana Henderson. Check it out later."

"You seem to have a song for every situation in life," Veronica remarks.

"Maybe," Olivia replies with a grin.

"You sing pretty well too."

"Thanks. And don't be scared. You'll be alright. Just try to enjoy the views," she reassures her.

They continue their boat ride. The shoreline opens up to a picturesque landscape. The water reflects the sky's serene blue, mirroring the fluffy white clouds that seem to stretch on forever. The surrounding greenery adds to the tranquil scene, with trees and bushes gently swaying in the light breeze. It's a moment of serene beauty, one that Veronica couldn't have imagined she would experience on this impulsive trip.

"What's the deal with Finn? He seems young to work as a receptionist." She reaches out to Olivia's ears with a loud voice again.

"He is the son of the owner. Her mother owns the motel. And most of the shops, restaurants, and motels you see here are run by locals. He does night shifts three times weekly."

"Does he go to school?"

"Yeah, he's in high school." Olivia takes a pause, then, in a mockingly funny way asks, "Why? Do you like him?"

She remains silent with a smile as if to get the joke, but inside her mind she says, "I wish you knew who I like."

"You should make me a playlist sometimes. On my phone. You've got great taste in music" Veronica says.

"Sure. I'll be glad to." Olivia glances around and then looks at her, asking, "Have you ever been on a boat and sailed around a lake?"

"Never," Veronica replies, meeting her eyes before gazing out at the water reflecting the sun. "This is my first time."

"Alright, stand up then."

"What do you mean?" Veronica asks nervously.

"Just stand up, and see what I see. You'll get a much better view if you stand and look around." Olivia takes her right hand again and guides her closer to the boat's steering wheel, standing alongside her.

She feels a mix of nerves and unease as she stands up while the boat moves, but her unease subsides somewhat as Olivia's delicate touch reassures her. Pulling her closer, Olivia whispers, "You only realise whether you're afraid of heights or not when you're up high."

They decide to dock their boat at a nearby restaurant. After arrival, they spot several boats and jet skis lined up in various rows. The atmosphere is less bustling compared to the summer months. The once-crowded swimming pool now sits nearly deserted. The interior of the restaurant catches their attention with elegant chandeliers and tastefully adorned furniture. The lunchtime crowd seems sparse, with only a couple and a trio of people occupying tables. They observe the couple who have just placed their order, leaving their table vacant for the moment. The trio nearby is engrossed in a meal arrayed with various dishes. They choose a table they find suitable. As the waiter approaches, they signal him over to place their orders. Veronica opts for a classic club sandwich with a side of French fries, while Olivia goes for a garden salad topped with grilled chicken. They both order beers to drink. The waiter jots down their choices and assures them that their meals will be served shortly. In the meantime, Veronica takes a pack of cigarettes out of her pocket. She looks over at Olivia and inquires about her interest in one. Olivia declines and instead watches as Veronica uses her lighter to light the cigarette.

She exhales a smoke while Olivia asks, "So how long have you decided to stay?"

"I haven't yet. But maybe six or seven days." She replies.

"You plan to go somewhere else or straight to home?"

"Home."

"So what's your last name? If you don't mind me asking?"

"Joyce."

"Veronica Joyce." Olivia says her name aloud. However, she enjoys how she pronounced it. When Olivia speaks her full name, it gives off a different feeling. It was probably something that she secretly yearned for. When it is satisfied, a new emotion rushes through her body.

"Do you know the origin of your name?"

"I don't know, Irish maybe. What's yours?"

"Rogers."

"Olivia Rogers. That sounds nice."

Olivia smiles and says, "It's German. My father told me that it means famous spearman."

"That's cool." She taps the ashes from her cigarette into the ashtray. "Hey, do you mind creating the playlist we talked about earlier?" She takes out her phone and hands it over to Olivia.

"Sure," Olivia replies.

Veronica's gaze lingers on her, smoke streaming from her cigarette, entranced by Olivia's presence, as her focus is diverted by the phone's screen. Less than a day have passed since their paths crossed, but the events unfolding in Olivia's company carry a weight that goes beyond regular hours. Her enticing energy appears to have created a mystical tether around Veronica, keeping her gaze fixed. Olivia's aura, which is woven with a captivating charm, appears to have encircled her within this fixed gaze, subtly hinting that there is no way to avoid the attraction that she exudes. When Olivia glances back at her, she shifts her gaze with a glimpse of shyness in her eyes.

Once Olivia has completed the playlist, the waiter brings their food and they start eating. Their continued playful banter creates a pleasant atmosphere. The nearby couple also seems to be having a good time, as their laughter briefly fills the restaurant. Once they finish their meal, Veronica takes out another cigarette. The lighter's flame casts a small, mesmerizing glow in its surroundings. The tobacco burns as she inhales the smoke. This time, when she offers Olivia a cigarette, she accepts.

"Do you smoke a lot?" Olivia asks.

"These days, I do."

"I like the way you light up cigarettes. It's hard to describe, but there's something captivating about it. It's almost like you're the protagonist in a film, and someone behind the scenes is capturing the perfect shot. It would make a remarkable scene."

"Speaking of shots, I actually brought a camera with me, but I haven't taken any pictures yet."

"You should definitely take some, especially when we go out next time."

Hearing the words "next time" fills Veronica with a subtle joy that remains unspoken with a secret emotion only her heart understands.

Olivia leans in, her elbows finding a comfortable spot on the table, her fingers delicately holding the cigarette, nails adorned with a shade of maroon. A soft waft of her perfume catches her attention. She is aware of that smell and is aware of its ability to evoke memories. She is conscious of the possibility for this scent to elicit a flood of memories, even decades later. It's like a connection between moments that transcends time and is just waiting to reappear at the first whiff of that comforting scent. One might forget their favorite book, cherished memories, or even beloved films, but the fragrance of their favorite person is something that remains unforgettable.

"So, do you have a brother or sister?" Olivia asks, exhaling a puff of smoke.

"A little brother. His name is Kevin."

"And what does he do?"

"Goes to high school and parties all the time. He's quite

the opposite of me. Always comfortable around people."

"Are you uncomfortable?"

"Sometimes."

"So you don't like people?"

"Not everyone, but I don't like most of them. I sometimes find people repulsive. Most of them pretend to care even if they don't, and it feels like we are living in a lie."

"I understand your point. But don't you think the fact that a person is sitting next to you but you don't know what is going on inside their head makes people interesting?"

She smiles and asks, "What's going on in your head?"

Olivia chuckles softly and replies, "Only if you knew."

That night, as she sits at her table with her diary open, she doesn't know where to start. The entire day was spent with Olivia, and it stirred emotions within her that she hadn't felt before. She's unsure of what to say when they meet again. Should she express her feelings? Should she admit how she can't take her eyes off her? Would it be too soon, given it's been just a day? Yet, there's a part of her that believes even without saying anything, Olivia understands. Every interaction they had, each moment they spent together, and every subtlety of Olivia's presence are all diligently recorded. A smile tugs at the corners of her lips as she uses her words.

She is aware that this smile has been with her the entire time she has been writing it, living not on her lips but in the centre of her heart. Is this what it's like to fall in love? Veronica muses, feeling in her heart what she has written on the pages. And at the end of the lines she adds, *"What is it that makes me feel this way? I don't know. All I know is that I have been looking for something or someone. And I have found that."*

Once she wraps up her writing, she rises from her seat and heads to the balcony. Just as she did the previous day, she settles into the chair, slips on her headphones, and navigates through her phone for a fitting song. Olivia's playlist comes to mind, and she realizes this is an ideal moment to give it a listen. The setting is reminiscent of yesterday, yet the emotions coursing through her now are more intense, more profound. Yesterday, she hadn't been gifted a personalized playlist by someone. She reflects briefly on how swiftly circumstances can shift.

CHAPTER FIVE

October

The sky was hazy in the middle of October. Through the mist, the sun's soft but warm rays could be seen. The trees were adorned with autumn-colored leaves, which contributed to the atmospheric dreaminess. A hint of coolness in the air made it ideal for cosy clothing. Through the fog, birds flew gracefully while their songs were muffled. It was a day where the brightness of summer and the cosiness of autumn collided. Everywhere had a certain air of mysticism, as though nature were revealing secrets through the mist.

They are supposed to meet on the streets, so Veronica went outside. she notices when she first arrives, the streets are deserted. Olivia's tardiness. She has been waiting for a while, but Olivia has yet to show up. Compared to yesterday, it feels much colder today. Over her shirt, she wore the sweater Olivia had lent her. However, it is still unable to warm her. She stands there waiting, but she is not dissatisfied. She has the impression that she could wait for Olivia all day without experiencing anything, as long as she shows up.

Olivia finally arrives, her steps quick, but an hour late. Seeing her, she felt relieved. Olivia was wearing a leather jacket while holding one with her hands folded.

"I'm really sorry," Olivia says, her breath slightly hurried from her quick walk. "And I realised it's colder today, so I brought one of my jackets for you. Just the sweater won't work in this weather." She hands Veronica the jacket, her eyes showing genuine concern.

Veronica smiles, touched by her thoughtfulness. "You didn't have to go through this trouble. Thank you." She takes the jacket and puts it on, feeling the warmth seep in. It's not just the jacket that warms her, but the thought that she cared about her. Oh, to be cared for by someone like her, she thinks.

They start walking together down the streets just like yesterday but today the sky was more overcasted by clouds of the fall.

"Is it better during the summer here?" Veronica asks.

"It depends on which season one likes. For me, I like winter, so I always anticipate it. Generally, people prefer to spend their vacation here in summer. So typically, anyone would say summer is better."

Veronica takes a glance at her while she speaks, and she listens to every word attentively. She wants to say it doesn't matter what others think; it only matters what you think, but she doesn't. It's almost like her heart speaks, but her mouth is silent.

"And you? Which season do you like?" Olivia asks this time.

"I like fall. October seems the best time for me to do anything."

Veronica has always thought fall was the best time. She used to wait for this time the whole year. There is some kind of different feeling in this season that she felt.

"Sounds like you," Olivia remarks, as if she knows exactly what she is trying to express. "Have you had breakfast?"

"No, I haven't," she admits. She had been so focused on meeting Olivia that she almost forgot about breakfast. The thought had crossed her mind earlier, but she had dismissed it, not wanting to risk being late.

"You should at least have some coffee. There's a coffee shop at the end of the street. Shall we go?"

"I'm okay, but if you insist, we can."

The cafe can be seen as they proceed down the street. It

has inviting displays of pastries in its windows, and the air is filled with the aroma of freshly ground coffee. Small outdoor seating area looks warm and inviting with colourful umbrellas. While enjoying their drinks and treats, customers can be heard conversing in a soft murmur. The espresso machine being used by a barista gives the environment a lively rhythm. The thought of a warm cup of coffee makes the chilly morning feel a little cosier as they both walk towards the cafe.

At the cafe, They step up to the counter, greeted by the friendly barista. They place their orders; Olivia opts for a cappuccino while Veronica goes for a simple black coffee. The barista's hands dance expertly over the machines as they prepare the drinks. With their coffee cups in hand, they find a comfortable spot at a corner table by the window. If the day was sunny, the warm sunlight would have filtered through the glass. The chatter of other patrons blends with the soft music playing in the background. Veronica reaches into her pocket and pulls out a cigarette. She lights it up. The tendrils of smoke curl upward, mingling with the air around them. She offers Olivia a cigarette, but she politely declines with a shake of her head.

"So you don't smoke much, it seems."

"I used to. But I started smoking less after getting into

college," Olivia replies with a casual tone. "Just trying a little bit of self-care, I guess."

"That makes sense. Taking care of yourself is important."

Olivia's attention drifts to the music playing in the café. "Do you know the tune that's playing?" she asks, indicating the piano melody in the background.

She listens for a moment. "No idea."

"They are playing just the piano version, but the original song has lyrics. It's 'Nani mo kikanaide' by Yumi Arai. A beautiful song, really."

"You seem to know a lot about Japan."

"Only what I've learned. Never been there though. I've always been fascinated by different cultures, Japan included. I find their music, art, and way of life very interesting."

"I like what I've heard so far here. What does it mean in English, though?" She asks curiously.

Olivia chuckles and playfully waves her hand. "Don't ask me anything."

"What?" she asks, confused.

"I was kidding. The title of the song is actually 'Don't ask me anything' in English," Olivia clarifies playfully before taking a sip of her coffee. She then asks, "Did you listen to my playlist?"

"Oh, yeah. I loved it. You've got great taste in music. I

enjoyed every track."

"I'm glad to know that." Olivia takes out her phone and earphones, placing her coffee cup aside. "Can I have your smoke?" she asks, focused on scrolling through her phone.

Veronica hands her the half-finished cigarette, watching as Olivia takes a drag. The cigarette had just touched her lips a few seconds ago, and now Olivia's lips are on the same spot. She can't help but feel a peculiar sensation, a mixture of connection and anticipation, as she observes Olivia smoke the same cigarette. The thought crosses her mind: Did Olivia intentionally refuse a cigarette earlier, only to smoke the same cigarette that she smoked?

"Come closer," Olivia suggests, removing the left earbud from her ears and offering it to her. Leaning in, resting her elbow on the table, she positions her head to insert the earphone into Veronica's ear. "Listen to this. It's the original song."

As they share the earphone, a faint wisp of smoke lingers in the air. With the same earphone in their ears, they become synchronized listeners, experiencing the same melody. The music travels from the device, through the wires, into their ears, and finally reaches their souls. The song playing is 'Don't Ask Me Anything' by Yumi Arai.

They leave the coffee shop. The day was still in its early stages. Veronica was unaware of any of her plans. Olivia simply instructed her to meet there immediately in the morning, and she did as she was instructed. She asked no questions at all. She had never before in her life felt such a strong desire to hang out with someone. The press conference they mentioned yesterday is this evening. What will they do the rest of the day? She believes Olivia must have plans.

"So, where to now?" She asks.

"Well, I'm taking you to a cool spot. We're gonna be joined by some other people. You're gonna love it."

"What? Who?"

The thought of meeting someone else doesn't really interest her. She would prefer to spend this time with her rather than anyone else. She's never been particularly drawn to meeting new people, finding most of them uninteresting. Her previous mention of finding people repulsive also reinforces her feelings. So why did Olivia decide to introduce her to others?

"You'll see. They're cool. You'll like them, don't worry."

She goes along with Olivia's plan, even if she's not entirely fond of the idea. As they walk, Veronica takes out her camera and snaps a few photos of the streets. It's the first time she's used her camera since leaving home. Olivia continues walking ahead. Veronica comes to a stop for a moment, unnoticed by her. When she eventually glances back, she finds Veronica standing there with the camera in her hands. A smile naturally forms on her face, and in that fleeting instant, before the moment vanishes, Veronica captures a candid photo of her. A photo means a lot to her. She still has photos of her grandma and her childhood kept in a picture book. And surely this capture will mean a lot to her too. She will keep this one forever, she believes. She takes multiple photos after that. Olivia is adamant about removing the camera from her grasp, and her resolve is apparent. She suggests that Veronica be the focus this time. Veronica strikes a position as instructed by her. Her eyes fixed forward. Through the clouds, the sun shines through, giving her face a soft glow. Olivia carefully adjusts her hair to fall just so as she reaches over. When everything is ready, Olivia takes her picture, stopping time in its tracks.

The path Olivia mentioned leads them back to the spot where Veronica had initially picked her up in her car. A narrow trail opens up into the woods from here. The lush greens covers the area, and the still streets combined with the overcast sky give rise to an atmosphere that is hauntingly beautiful. She had last entered the forest not far from where she had spent a day resting on her journey. That time, she went on a solo adventure and played in the rain. But as she enters the woods once more, she is not alone. Olivia's presence changes her perspective. She used to think that she preferred solitude to company, but after meeting her, she has changed her mind. She has only recently come to the conclusion that being with Olivia is preferable to being alone.

Arriving at the designated spot, Veronica's eyes fall upon a weathered wooden caravan house. Time has left its marks on it, evident in its aged appearance—perhaps a fixture here for a decade or more. The caravan is encircled by tall, lush trees, which create a spooky atmosphere. Positioned in front of the house are several couches, upon which three individuals are seated. A boy probably around his twenty and a girl, perhaps of the same age but seeming younger. Finn is among them, occupying one couch that faces the other two. The identities of these strangers remain unfamiliar to her.

Olivia strides forward, her presence noted first by Finn due to his position facing their direction. A friendly touch on the shoulder alerts them to her approach. With a jovial tone, she greets them, "What's up, guys?"

The girl voices her surprise, mentioning she thought Olivia might not make it. She dismisses that notion, introducing Veronica with a gesture. The pair turns their attention towards Veronica, offering friendly hellos. They rise from their seats, circling the couch to extend their hands for a handshake. The girl introduces herself as Michelle. Her left arm is adorned with intricate tattoos, and her nose and ears are adorned with multiple piercings. A tiny mole rests beneath her lower lip. The young man goes by Jonathan, standing at around six feet tall. A well-groomed mustache and beard accentuate his face. Veronica reciprocates their handshakes with a warm smile. They kindly invite her to take a seat, and she does so. Jonathan heads into the house and reappears with a six-pack of beer, distributing one to each of them. As they crack open their cans, he initiates the conversation.

"So, where are you coming from?" he inquires, turning his attention to Veronica.

"Columbus," she responds, popping the top of her can.

"I've been showing her around. But she won't be staying for long." Olivia chimes in, speaking on Veronica's behalf.

Michelle takes a sip of her beer before posing her question. "So, you came all by yourself?"

"Yeah. Just me."

"That's nice."

Veronica had anticipated more probing questions, perhaps about why she was alone or why she chose this place. Michelle's simple response unexpectedly put her at ease.

Finn was silent all this time. He didn't utter a word. That seems like a trait of his personality. He is oddly quiet. Doesn't seem to interrupt anyone's business and proceeds with the usual. Though he seems to be busy most the time with his phone.

Olivia shifts her gaze towards Veronica and starts telling her about the place, "So basically we hang around here most of the time. This is like a secret spot of ours since childhood. We grew up together and did all sorts of stuffs here. Now, Michelle and Jonathan lives here. The caravan house was owned by a man who lived here long ago I heard from my mom. He died one day and from then the house stayed just like it was. We re-arranged the house one day while we were here. I think I was in seventh grade back then. And yeah, that's how it has became a spot for us."

"Sounds great. How long have you been living here?" She asks to Michelle.

"One and a half year."

"You guys like it?"

"Definitely. We love it. It's quiet and nature all around. Free from everything. As a matter of fact, there's nothing to dislike here." Says Jonathan.

"What do you guys do then? How do you make a living?"

"We manage a pub close by. You really ought to check it out," Michelle responds. "He's a musician, too." While beaming at Jonathan, she continues, "He hasn't been signed by a label yet, but he's working on it."

"That's pretty cool. Are you on Spotify? What's your stage name?" Veronica asks Jonathan.

"Yeah, let me show you."

When Veronica hands him her phone, he opens Spotify and finds his music profile. She promises to make sure to listen to his music tonight. She thought both of them were nice people. They are nicer than most others out there, even though one might not think they are from a distance given their messy appearance. They appear to be a happy couple living the life of their dreams. In the woods, engaging in their favourite activities. watching out for one another. Many people envision a life like that.

"We had a band too in our teenage days," Olivia interjects. "That is something we had a passion for back then. I used to play bass, Jonathan sang and played rhythm guitar, while Michelle was on the lead guitar. And Finn here played drums. We used to play gigs in local bars and parties often."

"You didn't tell me that before. What was the name of the

band?" Veronica asks, curiously.

"Oh, don't ask, it was so cringe. The Cunts, we named it," Finn chimes in for the first time, and everyone bursts out in laughter.

"We grew up, and everyone went their own ways, you know. Even though we still live in the same town, we have our different paths. I started college, Finn took over the motel after his mom got sick, Michelle got busy with the bar. The band fell apart. So now it's only him who makes music." Olivia explains.

They kept talking and swapping stories as the minutes passed, the exchange flowing naturally. They cooked on a gas grill, and eventually they all sat down to eat lunch together while the scent of grilling meat filled the air. The ambiance was welcoming and unhurried. Finn rolled a joint afterwards, which all of them were smoking. The smoke surrounded the air around them. At first, she hesitates, but she doesn't anymore when Olivia asks her to try it out once. She had this tingly feeling at first, as if someone was trying to make her laugh; her mouth seemed stretched wide to laugh. But she also felt a sense of connection. Sharing moments like this with a group of people is something she has never done before. She thought this was out of her personality trait, and she doesn't like people, but the time spent with them will probably never be forgotten by her. This particular afternoon in October will always remain in her heart like a chapter of a memory that cannot be erased. It is just like Oliva told her, *"You only know whether you have a fear of heights or not when you are high above."*

CHAPTER SIX

The Writer

They enter the auditorium for the press event of the writer. They find that it is already underway. The interviewer and the writer are seated on the stage, engaged in conversation. The room is filled with students and eager fans, all leaning forward with anticipation. Veronica and Olivia made their way to the last row and take their seats. The writer, adorned in a light blue suit and a pearl necklace, is already speaking, her words capturing the audience's attention.

"It doesn't follow that you can't succeed. You cannot worry that no one will listen to or enjoy your music if you are a musician and you are creating it. You have to work for what you want. whatever happens. You will never get anywhere if you don't start because of the internal fear that grips you. When I wrote my first book, I, personally, gave a lot of consideration. Fear is one of the characteristics that describe me as a person. However, I kept reminding myself that I had to. And just look where I ended up. I'm now talking about my books while sitting in front of you and the audience."

The interviewer glanced down at her notes before posing the question, "So, where do you draw your inspiration for writing? Where do these ideas originate?"

"I believe that ideas are ever-present. As humans, we possess our senses, which are in a perpetual state of activity. The universe is brimming with countless elements, and within it, words and ideas exist. By listening intently and remaining observant, one might be fortunate enough to grasp hold of some of these fragments. Now, you might wonder why not everyone perceives the same words that I do. The world is a place of diversity, and not everyone shares the same thoughts or inclinations. Each individual's perception is unique. If I were to ask all of you to envision a person you aspire to become in the future, each response would differ. While perhaps one or two might bear similarities, the likelihood of them being identical is minimal. Thus, an individual will only hear the ideas that he or she desires. All forms of art and creativity, be it paintings, plays, poetry, literature, films, or dramas, are crafted from these fragments scattered throughout the universe. These fragments are seized by individuals who keenly observe their surroundings."

The interviewer clasps her palms together, and asks, "So what are your thoughts on failure, or perhaps I might say those who do not succeed even with determination?"

"The world is diverse, as I already have said, and that diversity opens up a wide range of opportunities. The possibility of failing to reach one's goals is one of those possibilities. I would advise knowing oneself in such circumstances. We are not equipped to handle every situation. However, the first step is to understand who we are. Self-awareness is the key to every door's unlocking. We must understand our own needs, wants, thoughts, desires, feelings, and preferences. How can we find our way if we lack this self-awareness? Yes, it is entirely possible that you have failed in your endeavours. However, there might be hidden causes for it that you haven't yet found. Certainly, let's consider a contradictory example. Imagine John is en route home and decides to hire a taxi. As he steps into the cab, he notices the driver appears slightly inebriated. Not overwhelmingly intoxicated, but John detects a subtle sign of it. Due to his alertness, he opts to leave the taxi, concerned that remaining inside might lead to an accident. However, upon exiting the taxi, an unforeseen event occurs: he is struck by another car from behind, resulting in his unfortunate death. In this instance, he attempted to avert a potential accident by leaving the taxi, only to find himself involved in a different accident. This narrative raises the notion that certain aspects of life seem entwined with destiny, events that unfold regardless of our immediate choices. The only destiny that is guaranteed is death. However, the realisation that you won't be on this planet forever is what makes life worthwhile. So accepting destiny is the key to contentment."

The auditorium remains enveloped in a profound silence, as if everyone is hanging on to the writer's every word with unwavering attention. The interviewer proceeds, "Many of your works are noted for their subtle touch of spirituality. Could you share your thoughts on that aspect of your writing?"

The writer slightly adjusts her sitting position as she replies, "Well, it appears that many people these days find spirituality to be a fascinating subject. But most people still don't fully understand what it means. Over the past few decades, the term 'spirituality' has expanded far beyond its original meaning and, obviously, beyond all forms of religion. Personally, I believe that the popularity of spirituality or the concept of spirituality among people these days is due to the diminished trust that people have in traditional sources of authority, such as politicians and religious leaders. Spirituality strikes me as a lofty concept. Additionally, it has to do with a person attempting to realise all of their potential. It is a source of authority as well, but it comes from within rather than from outside forces. similar to relying more on yourself than anything else."

"So, where did the term originate from?"

"The origin of the word 'spirituality'?" she clarifies.

"Yes, exactly."

"Well, it actually has its origins in the Christian vocabulary, where it initially denoted someone preoccupied solely with their own pleasure. Over time, it took on a more idealistic connotation."

"Where do you think the relationship between spirituality and religion fits in?"

"In my opinion, the core of every religion is spirituality. Because religion has become institutionalised, some people would dispute the argument. However, if you really think about it, every religion teaches the same thing. Many ancient philosophers also had it in their hearts. In addition to practising it, I think they were also fascinated by it."

"Do you think it's solely an individual concept or does it encompass collectivism as well?"

"I believe it's not solely individual. In modern times, it has gained social implications too. It's being used in various sectors like healthcare, business, leadership, and many others."

"Does it involve any kind of practises or similar things?"

"It includes a variety of techniques, including meditation. There are, however, many additional practises that go far beyond simple mental exercises. Physical body-related matters are also included in the realm of spirituality. It's actually applicable to circumstances in daily life. When thought about, even controlling one's anger and rage in a real-life situation can be regarded as a form of spiritual practise. It indicates a direction for meaning and greater enlightenment. You could also say that there is a desire for perfection. And that happens when something changes or transforms. Getting rid of negative, self-destructive behavioural patterns could be one example of this."

"So, is it holistic?"

"Naturally, it is. Not just my body, mind, or psyche are involved. Actually, it's about life as a whole. progressively coming to know who I am as a whole."

"Do you believe that religion is no longer necessary in today's world of increasing progress and evolving ideas? You also mentioned how people's mistrust of religious leaders is changing their sources of authority."

"I do not believe that in order to come up with progressive ideas, religion has to be eliminated. The message of every religion is the same. Its purpose is to direct people. to direct people in the direction of something and to provide meaning for it. The same thing is said by spirituality, and as I've previously stated, spirituality is at the heart of every religion. The only issue with it is that everyone in a belief system starts to believe they are in possession of the only true knowledge. And when you think that way, you begin to denigrate other beliefs and believe they are incorrect. That causes some unanticipated chaos among people of various religious beliefs. We must respect everyone's religious beliefs because the universe is filled with diverse cultures. The definitive truth is unknown to us. We are a part of a bigger as a whole. I'd advise being more perceptive and paying attention to your surroundings. Keep an eye on what's going on. Also, be open to progress and change. Accept new viewpoints."

"Your characters frequently struggle with existential and spiritual crises. How do you go about creating genuine and relatable experiences for them?"

"Authenticity is crucial in storytelling, in my opinion. I draw on my own experiences and observations, but I also conduct extensive research and speak with people who have travelled similar paths. To portray these experiences convincingly, it is necessary to delve deeply into the emotional and psychological aspects of them."

"How do you believe literature and storytelling can help readers reconnect with their spiritual side in a world that appears to be driven by materialism and external success?"

The author coughs to clear her throat and continues, "Literature has the uncanny ability to awaken dormant aspects of our inner selves. Readers can explore different perspectives, challenge their beliefs, and revive their sense of wonder and curiosity about life's deeper questions through storytelling. It provides a safe space for introspection and spiritual exploration, encouraging readers to set out on their own inner journeys."

"When it comes to their own spiritual journeys, many readers have found solace and inspiration in your books. What message or insight do you hope your work conveys to readers?"

"My greatest hope is that my stories resonate with and comfort readers, that they see a reflection of their own spiritual quests and gain new perspectives. If my writing can even elicit a brief moment of introspection or a deeper connection to their own spirituality, I consider it a meaningful success."

The interviewer reaches for a new note at the bottom of the stack of sheets she held. With a smile, she addressed Ms. Lucy, "So, Ms. Lucy, we've gathered some questions from the audience. Would you mind taking a moment to answer them?"

Ms. Lucy's expression remained warm as she responded, "Of course not. I'd be happy to. Please go ahead and proceed with the questions."

"What is the advice that you would likely give to the youth of today? This was asked by Simon Ferris."

The writer's gaze shifted towards the attentive audience before her as she responded, her voice carrying a mix of earnestness and encouragement, "Look, most of you sitting here today, right in front of me, are young. In fact, the majority of my readers fall within the young demographic. Many of you are probably in the range of eighteen to twenty-one or thereabouts. This phase of life you're in right now, it's the pinnacle, the highlight. My advice to you? Embrace and relish your youth. It's an invaluable gift, not to be squandered."

She paused for a moment, her eyes scanning the eager faces before continuing, "I understand that a lot of you are harboring aspirations, dreams of starting something meaningful. But often, procrastination creeps in, halting your progress. That's not the path you should tread. Be unapologetically true to yourself, and pursue what sets your heart on fire. As long as your actions don't cause harm to others, you have the freedom to explore any avenue you wish."

Leaning forward, her words grew more impassioned, "The reality of the world today is that some of you might find yourselves in corporate roles five years down the line, while others might chart their own course as entrepreneurs or in similar roles. Regardless of the path you take, responsibilities will naturally come knocking. And believe it or not, in the blink of an eye, you'll find yourself standing right where you once dreamed of being. So, make the most of this golden period of youth by infusing it with fun and passion. If you're envisioning yourself fronting a rock 'n' roll band, don't hesitate—just go for it. Craving the electric guitar prowess of a Jimmy Page? Take the plunge; you've got what it takes. Aspire to channel your inner Alex Turner? Believe me, you already are him; all it takes is that first step. So, dream grandly, let your ambitions soar, and relentlessly pursue those aspirations while the fire of youth burns brightly within you."

The audience's enthusiastic applause now reverberated throughout the once-quiet auditorium. Her words had an undeniable spark to them that managed to awaken the youthful spirit in everyone in the room. The air seemed to change as a fresh sense of inspiration spread like wildfire. She calmly and gently answered each of the additional questions that were asked after that stirring speech. The speaker's undeniable charm continued to enthral Veronica as the meeting went on. Veronica was drawn in and profoundly moved by the wisdom being shared because of the speaker's words because they had a special power.

When they left the event, it was getting close to 9:00 p.m. The streets outside of the university's immediate vicinity were calm as usual. The pathways were lit by a sparse smattering of lampposts, creating soft pools of light amidst the darkness. The calm scene was briefly disturbed by a middle-aged woman riding her scooter by.

"So, did you like what she said?" asks Olivia.

"Her words were complex, but they served a purpose. I must say I'm impressed."

"I'm going to lend a few books of hers to you. You should give them a read."

"Sure, I'll be glad to."

They walk in silence for a while, side by side. Veronica interrupts by saying, "Do you meet a lot of people here?"

"I do. It's a place where people come and go every time, you know. And I work at the coffee shop there, so yeah, obviously I see a lot of people. I meet a lot of them."

"That's nice. Must be great."

A part of her starts to wonder if she has ever hung out with someone else like she's doing now. Is it just a friendly gesture to a tourist that she's making? Or maybe she's just overthinking the whole thing in her mind. Making things up. But her confusion breaks as Olivia whispers, "But I haven't hung out with someone else for two days straight, like I'm doing with you now."

A slender smile forms on her lips as she hears that. She feels comfortable enough just from the words. The two of them continues to move silently along the narrow path that was dimly lit.

CHAPTER SEVEN

Limerence

For Veronica, the nights seemed to go on forever. Every second seemed to drag on, as if time had slowed down. On the other hand, the days appeared to vanish almost as quickly as they arrived, like morning mist. Her mind was constantly racing with ideas and expectations for the upcoming day during these longer nights. As Olivia's image danced through her mind, a soft warmth spread through her, resulting in the unintentional curve of a smile. She was now engulfed in an uncharted emotional landscape as a result of this strange sensation, a blending of excitement and unfamiliarity. The time she spent with Olivia seemed to fly by like sand grains in stark contrast to the leisurely pace of her nights. It was as if time itself decided to speed up when she was with her while slowing down elsewhere. This feeling brought back memories of her childhood summers, when the eagerly awaited break from school finally came. Plans would be eagerly made, but in reality, the days would fly by at a breakneck pace, frequently leaving those plans unfulfilled. But for Veronica, this particular experience was different from her usual ones. Instead of being swept away by the speed of time, she discovered herself in a period where everything went as planned and where each conversation and shared experience felt as though it had been predetermined by destiny. She never stops thinking about Olivia. She can still clearly recall every detail of that day in the boat, the first day they drove, and the peaceful nighttime street walk. She almost feels as though a completely new world has appeared all around her. Before she came here, she lived in a world that was entirely focused on her; now, however, two worlds have merged into one and are no longer distinct.

Veronica follows her routine every morning. She gets dressed and walks over to Olivia's workplace. She takes a seat and orders a coffee while holding a paperback. Her favourite past time has always been reading, which has captured her attention more than anything else. Surprisingly, she maintained her focus despite her surroundings being busy. But she finds it difficult to focus in this relatively calm environment. Her attention frequently wanders to the counter where Olivia is seated instead of staying focused on the text on the pages. When their gazes locked, smiles would naturally grace their lips, occasionally accompanied by a friendly wave. They'd stroll together along the serene streets, Veronica comfortably wrapped in the sweater gifted by Olivia while she wore her own.

They observed the delicate transition between day and night while perched on the promenade next to the lake. Even though there were no boats in the area, the water reflected the peace. Nevertheless, they could hear the distant murmur of an engine. Both had cigarettes in hand.

Veronica's voice blends in with the calm environment. "Have you ever experienced that feeling where you listen to a particular song repeatedly during a certain phase of your life, and then you suddenly stop?" She pauses to inhale from the cigarette before continuing, "And then, after a year or longer, that same song shuffles into your playlist, triggering a flood of memories as if you're time-travelling. Does that ever happen with you?"

Olivia turns to fully face her and responds, "I haven't experienced it exactly that way, but I do have certain songs that remind me of specific people. It's kind of similar to what you're describing, but instead of recalling memories of a particular time, it's more about associating the song with a specific person I shared those memories with. For instance, whenever I listen to 'Yesterday' by The Beatles, it immediately brings back memories of my mom, because she used to play that song a lot."

"She was a fan of The Beatles?"

"I wouldn't say a fan, because that was the only song I remember her playing from them. Maybe she had her own memories associated with that song."

Veronica remains silent.

Olivia continues, "She was more of a blues enthusiast. She adored blues music. Old blues records were her favorite. Jimi Hendrix, Albert Collins, Janis Joplin, T-Bone Walker – she played their records repeatedly."

For a moment, she considers sharing about her grandmother, but for some unknown reason, she refrains. Instead, she asks, "Do you believe in afterlife?"

"I wouldn't say I firmly believe in it, but there's a vast amount of unknowns out there. It could be one of those."

"It's just so strange when you really think about it."

"What, the afterlife?"

"That too. And also the fact that Earth has existed for billions of years, but our own existence is limited to just sixty or seventy years. What came before my existence is a mystery to me. I can only comprehend what's right here in front of me. And just like that, we'll be gone one day. No longer will we be aware of what is happening on Earth. The memory of us will be lost. It reminds me of a film, you know. It starts off at one place and ends up somewhere else. We still don't know what happened before or what will happen next, though."

"Well, then the ending matters, right?"

"How?"

"Like you said, life is similar to a film. So if it's a film, then obviously the ending holds more significance than anything else. Having a happy ending in life is important." Olivia says with a smile.

Olivia talks about performance art with a passion that is obvious. As she describes the intricate ways artists express themselves through this medium, her eyes brighten and her gestures take on an animated quality. Veronica, on the other hand, is conscious of the fact that she has never explored the world of performance art. She has never tried it, or felt interested in it, so her interest is aroused by Olivia's enthusiasm. She suggests a plan to further acquaint Veronica with this form of expression. She suggests them to go to a performance art presentation at the university theatre. Olivia thinks it's a great chance for her to experience performance art firsthand, given that such events are frequently held.

The campus is embraced by the waning daylight as they approach the university theatre. Conversations among the gathered people blend in with the sound of rustling leaves. Warm interior lighting creates inviting shadows at the theater's entrance. As attendees pour in, they take their seats as excitement permeates the room. The canvas of the stage is ready and waiting for the evening's performance. Olivia leads her through the crowd as they search for seats. The show begins as the lights start to fade and the first musical notes echo. Two figures appear on the stage in the low light, moving deliberately and in unison. One is clad in a swaying robe, while the other is wearing a metallic suit. The performer in robes unfolds a piece of paper and makes dramatic gestures while reading its contents. The person wearing the metallic suit, meanwhile, manoeuvres with mechanical accuracy while angling their body. The performers interact as spoken words and background music meld together, their facial expressions expressing a variety of emotions. They are suddenly surrounded by a projection of whirling hues. The movements of the pair become more vigorous, building to a mesmerising dance of contrasts that pits fluidity against rigidity and light against darkness. The show abruptly ends, leaving the audience in quiet contemplation.

The stage transforms, a stark contrast from the previous act. A single spotlight reveals a figure seated at a grand piano, fingers poised above the keys. The melody that emerges is haunting, evoking emotions that linger in the air. As the pianist's hands dance, a screen behind them comes to life with a series of vivid abstract visuals – splashes of color and intricate patterns. The music intensifies, building into a crescendo that reverberates through the theatre. Suddenly, a dancer appears, her movements echoing the rhythm of the piano. Her steps are sharp and precise, a dynamic contrast to the piano's melancholic melody. The interaction between the two intensifies, a dialogue between sound and movement. The dancer's motions become more frenetic, the piano's notes more urgent. Then, as if in a final plea, both the music and dance reach a climactic peak before abruptly falling silent. The dancer freezes, the pianist's hands hover above the keys, and the screen fades to black. The audience sits in reverent silence, moved by the powerful fusion of sound, visuals, and movement.

Unexpectedly, Veronica finds herself drawn to the performances. These new experiences are being revealed to her. Her thoughts ruminate on the dedication and work that went into producing such faultless performances, wondering about the meticulous rehearsals, the artistic vision, and the unwavering dedication. For her, it is a brand-new world, one that sparks her curiosity and sense of wonder.

They decide to have a drink after the performances are over before going to a nearby art gallery. They let their eyes wander through the varied collection of artworks as they strolled through the gallery's calm hallways. As they move along, they have hushed conversations while discussing the objects they see. They take their time, stopping in front of each piece of art to let the visual stories play out in front of them. The walls are covered in paintings, each one a window into the world of the creator. The gracefully posed sculptures beckon touch and exploration. Even though their fingers occasionally itch to trace the contours, they are content to respectfully observe. Bold strokes are placed in contrast to delicate lines, and colours blend harmoniously. Strokes and shades are used to depict emotions and expressions in works of art that freeze moments in time. Each piece of art performs in the gallery, triggering feelings that are often difficult to express with words. They visit all exhibit in turn as they leisurely explore. It is a silent dance of observation and reflection, with the audience listening intently for the unspoken conversations while the art tells its stories in silence.

"Hey, I have an idea," Olivia says, reaching for Veronica's drink and holding it in her hands. "No, maybe you should finish it," she adds with a smile, then hands the glass back to Veronica. They both raise their glasses, sharing a fleeting gaze before sipping the remaining contents together. The glasses are gently placed aside, and then their eyes meet again, their focus solely on each other.

"Okay, so the first rule is, no matter what, you can't laugh. Alright?" Olivia says with a cheerful glow in her eyes.

Veronica nods in agreement.

"And you're going to mimic everything I do, every single thing. Every facial expression, every gesture. Got it?"

"Okay."

"And as it continues, I'll start mimicking you back. So you won't be able to tell who's starting and who's following. And in that way, we'll create art."

They both take a deep breath and stand straight, facing each other. Despite their efforts, they eventually burst into laughter.

"No laughing! Be serious," Olivia scolds gently.

"Alright. Here it goes."

1Their facial expressions change, becoming intensely

serious. Their shared resolve is visible in the way their eyes lock. The palm of Olivia's left hand, which is mirroring Veronica's extended right hand, starts a graceful movement to the right. Their fingers are close, seperated by only the ethereal line of anticipation standing between them. Veronica embraces the imitation dance, breathing as naturally in time with Olivia as she moves. They both raise their heads at the same time, looking upward as if being pulled by invisible threads. It's a silent agreement to echo each other's nuanced expressions, an orchestration of connection. With a whispered breath, Olivia leans forward, closing the gap between them. Faces mere inches apart, they embark on a voyage of expressions, their countenances alternating between elation, solemnity, curiosity, and tenderness. Time seems to suspend, allowing these delicate exchanges to flourish and intermingle. They then lean back gracefully, increasing their separation while also deepening their harmony. As they set out on an unfamiliar voyage, their right hands weave a story of unity through the air. The synchronisation and flow are mesmerizing—clear yet hazy, as if their souls are exchanging secrets that their forms are merely echoing.

Every gesture, every inflection, merges seamlessly. The ephemerality of the moment melds with the enduring connection they're forging. Who leads and who follows becomes irrelevant, as if their hearts beat in the same rhythm, their souls dance to the same tune. They create a narrative of unity in this private act of collaborative creativity, a tale of intimacy told through gestures, expressions, and movements. A private performance that was unveiled in the privacy of the art gallery goes beyond simple imitation. An ephemeral masterpiece emerges from their souls whispering and bodies echoing, delicate yet resilient—a performance that requires no stage, only the intertwined hearts of two artists.

Veronica withdraws to her room and dons more cosy clothing. She is attempting to read while lying on her bed with a book. But she struggles to concentrate once more. Even though Olivia isn't there in person, she is thinking a lot about what has happened today and their shared experiences. Her touch has an exceptional feel. It's clear at this point that she is taken in by her. It has become difficult to resist the pull that has developed into the attraction.

She picks up the sweater Olivia had given her from the wall hanger and brings it back to bed with her. As she lies down, she holds the sweater close, taking a whiff. Despite wearing it briefly herself, the lingering scent still carries her perfume. It's as if she's wrapped in her essence, feeling embraced by her very presence. With the sweater pressed against her face, she inhales deeply, letting Olivia's scent envelop her. A languid sensation spreads through her lower body, awakening a slow burn of desire. Her body responds, her nipples tingling and stiffening in response to the intoxicating attraction. Overwhelmed by the intensity of her longing, she surrenders to her desires, her fingers slipping inside her shorts to explore the depths of her longing with a fervent touch. Soft, breathy moans escape her lips, filling the silent room with the sound of her escalating passion. Her movements grow more urgent, driven by an irresistible force. As time bends to the rhythm of her fervour, her intensity builds, creating the feeling of pleasure that surges through her body—a powerful release of the desire that consumed her. As her body gradually eases, a sense of calm and satiation washes over her, leaving her content.

CHAPTER EIGHT
SAPPHO

Since early morning, a dark wrap has been raised over the day by persistent rain. Veronica is awakened from sleep by the sound of raindrops pattering on the windowpane; their rhythm is like a constant lullaby. Outside, an intense downpour of rain is falling, swallowing the entire world in a depressing embrace. The lake, which was once calm, now trembles with the impact of raindrop, the relentless downpour distorting the surface. The world is shrouded in a layer of profound darkness as the sky above is covered in heavy clouds.

Veronica gets out of bed and the weight of the soaked day clings to her mind. She quickly gets dressed and freshens up before going downstairs. Finn is there, sitting in a startlingly familiar position, looking intently at his phone, and adopting the exact stance she had previously noticed. She can't help but wonder if he ever raises his eyes to look outside the glow of that screen or if his entire world is confined to it.

"Good morning, Finn." She greets him and sits on the couch that was kept beside the reception table.

Finn looks up and waves to her, "Hey, morning."

"How's it going?"

"Just usual. How 'bout you?"

"Great."

"Seems like you've been hanging around a lot with Olivia lately."

"Yeah. She's fun. She's showing me around, taking me to places."

"You're enjoying?"

"So far, yes. I've seen nice places out here. And you know what, I kinda wish I lived here."

For some reason, she feels at ease talking with Finn today. She doesn't feel like oversharing or making a gesture to impress him. She just feels as if he is a secure person to talk to. And she realises unconsciously that she has started to value the form of human connection.

"I suppose you might change your tune once you're settled in here."

"And why's that?"

"No particular reason." He responds with a nonchalant

shrug. "This place just doesn't do it for me. It's dull, in my opinion. I've got this itch to escape."

"Maybe we're blind to what's right in front of us."

"Maybe."

For a brief moment, they are encircled in silence. Finn resumes his habitual phone scrolling, while the gentle pitter-patter of rain continues. A gust of wind blows by now and then, carrying an almost tempestuous undertone with it. Veronica sparks up a cigarette and extends the offer to Finn. He nods in agreement, and she tosses the lighter and a cigarette to him, deftly caught in his grasp.

"You still play the drums?" Veronica asks.

"Not at all. I haven't had much time for anything since starting to work here. It's been difficult, especially since my mother became ill," Finn responds.

"What happened to your mum?"

"Osteoporosis." After a brief pause, he continues, his gaze fixed on her. "The doctor says she's going to need a lot of rest."

"Is this a serious condition?"

"It's not that serious. She is taking medication, which should help, but she must exercise caution to avoid injuries and accidents. Resting is thus the better option for her."

"Sounds better."

"You've been to the pub yet?" Finn asks.

"Which one?" she replies, momentarily confused before recalling, "Oh, Michelle's? No, not yet. We were thinking of going tonight, but it seems the rain might be sticking around for a while. Who knows, it might last all day."

"Usually it doesn't rain much during this season. The weather's been quite strange lately." Finn remarks.

"Seems like it," Veronica agrees. She gets up and stubs out her cigarette on the reception table's ashtray, then sits back on the couch. Looking at Finn, she asks, "Do you have any siblings?"

"No, it's just me. Why do you ask?"

"Just curious."

The rain continues to fall steadily throughout the afternoon, transforming the urban landscape into gleaming pathways and gleaming pavements. As evening falls, a new canvas emerges in the sky: a delicate fusion of soft oranges and muted yellows. This ethereal palette appears when a long day of rain finally gives way to a clear sky. The show is nothing short of magical, evoking a peaceful and wistful atmosphere. For Veronica, this one-of-a-kind sky carries a subtle hint of melancholy nostalgia, transporting her to moments and memories that seem both distant and cherished. A gentle ache begins to unfurl within her, a quiet longing for the familiarity of her own home. She yearns for the subtle fragrance that surrounds her room—a blend of comfort, memories, and the essence of time spent. Journeys have a peculiar way of teaching you new things and revealing the value of sights you once took for granted. The realisation dawns that the landscapes that frame your existence are not just mere backdrops; they're indispensable parts of your narrative. As days stretch and paths diverge, people evolve, and the world around you undergoes its own metamorphosis, sometimes so subtle you barely notice. The moments that you once thought were static and unchanging prove to be as transient as the clouds drifting across the evening sky. And in this yearning for the familiar, she recognises the evanescent nature of time itself. And then there's that distinctive scent— the embodiment of her dwelling place. Homes possess a unique olfactory identity, a blend of the lives lived within their walls. It's a scent that carries the echoes of shared meals, laughter, tears, and dreams woven into the fabric of everyday life. And as the twilight sky bathes everything in a soft glow, she can almost catch that scent, as if it's carried on the wind, reminding her of her roots and the essence of belonging.

She hears the bell ring while she is absorbed in her

thoughts. When she opens the door, she sees Olivia standing there with a smile on her face, wearing a long leather coat.

"Hey! I thought you weren't coming today." She says, she was surprised.

"Well, here I am. May I take you out, my lady?" Olivia replies with a sarcastic tone.

They both share laughter together as she invites her in.

"How's the room? You're comfortable?" Olivia asks as she looks around while sitting on the bed.

"Yeah, it's great. The view from the balcony is mesmerising. I like the quiet atmosphere." She replies.

As she gets busy dressing herself up and doing her hair, Olivia goes to her table and checks out the books that are kept there. Once she's ready and appears in front of Olivia, she takes a long glance at her as if she were looking at someone who mesmerised her for a moment. Even though she doesn't utter a word about that, Veronica understands.

"So, where do you want to go tonight? Should we go to a pub with soft music or a night club? Do you want to dance?" Olivia asks.

"I don't know. Wherever you take me. I just wanna spend more time with you."

The sound of raindrops echoed in the air as they drive to

Michelle's pub. The road has a wet sheen to it, made slick by the earlier downpour. The wind has a chill to it, as if it is a lingering remnant of the storm. Tree leaves cradle beads of water alongside the street, a gentle proof to the rain's recent visitation. Every single lush leaf seems to be a miniature reservoir holding a suspended memory of the rain that has now touched the plant life.

They leave the car and walk into the pub. The lights are turned down low. The seating is set up in a booth style. A band is playing music around the corner. Some people have gathered close to the stage, standing and watching them perform. She had never heard of the song. It wasn't overly heavy. Something along the lines of progressive rock. The lead singer has a buzzcut and appears to be in his twenties. The bassist and guitarist both appear to be teenagers. The girl on the drums is also the same. She has a tattoo on her neck. Michelle is behind the bar, mixing drinks and serving customers in the midst of a lively atmosphere. They walk over to her.

"Hey!" Olivia's voice rises above the din, a cheerful greeting competing for attention.

"Hello, ladies!" Michelle responds, her eyes warm despite the busy surroundings. "How are you guys?"

"Great. She wanted to see your pub, so I just brought her here." Olivia says, nodding to Veronica.

"I like it here. The band is nice." Veronica adds, a smile tugging at her lips.

"You do? Alright then. What are you ladies having tonight? It's totally on the house." Michelle offers to show her hospitality.

Olivia takes the lead in ordering, "I'll have a Mojito, please."

Veronica chimes in, "I'll go for a Cosmopolitan."

As the orders are placed, they take their seats in one of the booths, sinking into the atmosphere of the pub. The band starts to cover U2's 'With or Without You'.

"I know this song, it's one of my favorites." She says with a smile, her attention turning towards the band as they begin playing.

Olivia, slightly puzzled asks, "What song is this?"

She looks back at Olivia, surprised, and says, "What? You don't know U2? I thought you knew."

With a casual shrug, Olivia responds, "Well, I can't simply know all the bands around the world."

Veronica chuckles softly and insists, "The song's called 'With or Without You.' Listen to it."

During the second verse, she leads Olivia closer to the

stage, wanting her to get a better sense of the song and the band's performance. The singer's voice has a perfect tone and demonstrates the emotion of the lyrics. The bass lines pulse with rhythm, harmonising with the melody. Olivia leans in closer to her, admitting, "I think I've heard it before, but I didn't know the title or the band."

They immerse themselves in the song and the live performance side by side. She leans in and whispers to Olivia that this is her favourite part of the song as the music builds to the final bridge.

They left the pub a little tipsy. The previous wetness in the air, reminiscent of recent rain, has now transformed into a different kind of darkness. The peaceful setting contrasts sharply with the lively world they left behind inside the pub. The raindrops have finished their journey down the leaves. The streets tell an uneven story of the recent rain, with some patches now dry underfoot and others reflecting the dim streetlights with pools of rainwater. It's as if the dampness has been absorbed by the night, welcoming a sense of calm to settle over the town. This is the kind of atmosphere Veronica adored. And now that she's in that environment with her favourite person, the feeling only intensifies.

They take a walk instead of driving, navigating the streets

with a gentle unsteadiness, the evening's intoxication still lingering in their veins. A series of conversations unfolds between them as they walk, like a fabric created with words.

"You know I love the moment when it rains in the afternoon and the sky starts to clear just before the evening, it creates a similar to yellow wave on the sky which really looks beautiful," Veronica says, breaking the peaceful night air.

Olivia always listens carefully when she explains something. She has always been a good listener so far. "I like that colour too. I also like fog in general."

"I like the morning fog," she continues after a pause, "Don't you think it's more amazing to look at the raindrops while closing your eyes without looking at them?"

Olivia stops for a moment hearing that and glances at her, saying, "You amaze me." She continues walking alongside after saying that.

Veronica again continues her views as if she has found someone to share everything with.

"You know, I also like the sound of waves. I realised it recently. The sound of waves makes me nostalgic about a time that I've never been to. I don't know what this is, but this is a strange feeling that comes to me with the sound of the waves. If I pay attention to it, it transports me to a different realm of time. At least that's what it feels like to me."

Olivia falls into a thoughtful silence for a brief moment. Within her, a part of her consciousness wrestles with the notion of whether her words are just a result of her being drunk or if they unveil thoughts that have been confined for far too long. Could it be that this flood of thoughts has been bottled up within her, waiting for the right moment to emerge? Perhaps, she muses, it's the newfound sense of security between them that allows this torrent of emotions to spill forth. When she first met her, it struck her that she might be a quiet person. It's the quiet people who have millions of thoughts inside their heads but no one to share them with.

Their steps echo through the damp streets. An unexpected spark ignites within Olivia. Abruptly, she bursts into a spirited run, her laughter echoing through the air, a burst of uninhibited glee. Veronica's surprise propels her into motion, racing after her friend, a mixture of confusion and amusement spilling from her lips in a joyful uproar.

"Hey, wait up! What's gotten into you?"

Olivia glances back, her eyes dancing with joy, her laughter a tantalizing siren's call that she can't resist. Every trace of hesitation vanishes as her gaze lingers on Olivia's radiant face. Time itself seems to falter, every movement of Olivia's exuding an almost ethereal grace. It's as though the universe has conspired to cast their lives as a mesmerizing cinematic spectacle.

Their run ends in exhilarating laughing, and the sound of their laughter can be heard echoing through the quiet neighbourhoods. The world briefly becomes smaller as they turn a corner, their breaths blending together and their heartbeats beating in one. Olivia extends her arm, and Veronica is gently pushed up against the chilly brick wall by her forceful yet gentle touch. She is left reeling, her heart racing, and an array of feelings vibrating through her body as their lips meet like a fateful bridge between friendship and desire.

When they get to Olivia's house, something changes that eliminates any remaining space between them. As the area gets smaller, the boundaries melt away into the river like raindrops. Their bodies intertwine with an ancient passion and an intimacy that goes beyond simple physicality. Their bodies merge in a way that is impossible to explain as the warmth of their embrace covers them. Lips touch with a rush and familiarity that suggest an attachment that goes much deeper than what's visible to the outside world, as if they have done it many times before. Her heart beats with a rhythm of awareness as she experiences a discovery that is portrayed in the hues of a thousand different emotions. They've both privately studied the language of the kiss, and in this frail situation, they can now speak it with ease.

Layers—both literal and metaphorical—fall away as they lie back on the bed. They dissolve into one other's arms after removing their clothes and baring their vulnerabilities. Their loves flow with grace and abandon on this hallowed canvas as the art of love unfolds. Pen whispered affirmations that are etched into flesh by the fingers, creating sparkles that dance like fireflies at night. Their bond is a tune made up of soft whispers, loving touches, and the implicit promise of being fully present. Every touch contains an infinite amount of emotion and a hushed promise of an unwritten future. They paint portraits of one another on their bodies as the night draws in, their canvas a hallowed haven of shared aspirations and fresh insights. The walls that formerly divided them fall away in this dance of the souls, leaving only the gorgeous mosaic of their love.

Olivia grabs a cigarette from the table next to the bed. She fails to light it. She presses the lighter while maintaining the ciggarette between Veronica's lips. She takes the cigarette out of her mouth, lights it, and smokes before kissing Veronica on the forehead. A short while later, Veronica lights one for herself. She also grabs the book that rests on the table. The title says, 'The Poetry of Sappho,' catches her eye. Her gaze scanned the book's pages with interest. She would pause for a moment at certain verses, her thoughts delving into the text's intricate nuances. Then she'd turn the pages again, navigating the sea of words and ideas as she absorbed the wisdom of the poetry flowing through the book's pages. Olivia leans her head against Veronica's shoulder and softly whispers, "Read me something."

Opening the book to a random page, She begins to read in a gentle voice,

> 'As the stars surrounding the lovely moon will
>
> hide away the splendor of their appearance
>
> when in all her fullness she shines the brightest
>
> over the whole earth'

CHAPTER NINE
Melting

The cycle of good days eventually reaches its end. Veronica is acutely aware that she can't remain in this moment forever. Sooner or later, she would have to depart. The prospect of leaving tugs at her heartstrings, leaving an emptiness in its wake. Yet, among these feelings, there's also an optimistic and thankful corner within her. Every event, every emotion, and every encounter have been woven into the fragment of her life. She was in pursuit of something elusive, a puzzle piece, and now it feels like her path has been illuminated by the missing fragment like a bright light at the end of a dark tunnel.

She's sitting on a park bench with Olivia. The morning is lively. This is probably a place here that is louder than others. It's not as loud as her neighbourhood park, but compared to the streets and quiet nature here, it's livelier.

"So what are you going to do once you're back home? Olivia asks as she scans the area in front, where a few children can be seen playing at a distance.

"I don't know. Maybe the usual She replies.

"Are you going to decide which college to apply to or not?"

"I'm still not sure about that." She crosses her legs and adjusts them as a gentle wind blows through her hair. "A part of me tells me to go and start a new life. To do something better than I'm doing now. Have a degree; get a stable job, you know. Another part of me tells me to be easygoing and go with the flow. Be how I am now. I wish I could just stay here. With you. And forget the rest of the world."

Olivia takes her gaze back at her, and with a smile, she puts her soft hands over her hand. "I'll wait for you. I know you're going to come back. If you don't, I will come to you. We can always start the life that we want. You don't have to worry about that. Before that, you should figure out what you're going to do for now."

They are surrounded by a momentary silence that lasts longer than their spoken words. Her words have caused Veronica to feel a flurry of mixed emotions, and she is unsure of how to deal with them. Her heart is racing, and her mind is racing as if a strong current is rushing through her body.

The urgency of the situation hangs in the air, but their shared silence is peaceful—almost sacred. Her gaze shifts from the children to Olivia's calm expression. She doesn't have to say anything; the connection between them seems to be held in her eyes alone. Words aren't necessary in this quiet place; it seems as though their souls are conversing silently in a way that goes beyond words. They haven't said the word love yet, but it appears to be the most prevalent among them. The moment stretches on as the breeze carries the soft whisper of leaves and the distant laughter of children.

The day began with a gloomy sky, but as it went on, the sun emerged and made the town appear brighter. Veronica appears to be busy getting ready to leave for home. She plans to be home by tomorrow morning when she departs in the afternoon. The bittersweet feeling of farewell filled her heart. But she knows she wants to come back sooner or later because her treasure lies here. And the words she heard from Olivia about her waiting as long as it takes still soothe her soul.

When she gets to the reception, she sees Finn occupied with his regular duties.

"Hey, Finn!" she exclaims. "It's time to say goodbye."

He looks up, surprised. "You're leaving already? I thought

you were going to stay a little longer."

"Well, sooner or later, I had to leave, I guess. I feel it's the right time. But I do plan to return soon. Part of me will always remain here."

"Obviously, I know that." Finn responds with a chuckle.

This is the first time Veronica has seen Finn laugh. It's as if he's transformed into a completely different person. She briefly ponders whether she herself becomes a different person when she laughs.

Olivia stands in front of her parked car, ready to say her final farewell. She can sense the ache in her heart despite her face's lack of sadness. She hands her the bag, which she carefully places in the backseat. Olivia stretches her arms out and pulls her into a hug as the departure time approaches. The embrace lingers, a tight and lingering hug, as if they both feel the weight of this parting, as if it could be their final meeting.

"Drive safe." says Olivia. "Make sure to text or call me once you're home, alright?"

"I will. Don't worry. I will see you again, won't I?"

Olivia smiled at her and says, "Of course you will."

She realises it was a stupid question because she will see her again. She is convinced.

The vehicle begins to move slowly. Olivia stands there,

staring at it as it fades away. Her appearance is reflected in the rearview mirror. Veronica hopes to return here someday because she longs for it. She craves her touch, embrace, and words. She longs for every moment she has spent with her.

On her way home, she reminisces about her time there. It's almost as if all of her memories are flashing back to her. This time, the driveway appears to be easier for her. She realises that a lot has changed in her in just a few days. The fear and trepidation she felt when she began her journey are no longer present. Even the streets have become familiar to her. She has no intention of stopping in the middle and resting this time. She only comes to a halt to get petrol for her car. On her way, she listens to music from her playlist. There's this thing about music, she thinks, that even when you're alone and have no one to talk to, music speaks, it speaks the language of your soul. The smokes she exhales fly out the window and vanish with the wind. Several cars pass her briefly, but she is unconcerned. Even on an empty street, she would maintain a constant speed. It's not like she's afraid of getting into a car accident. It's just that she doesn't want to speed up. She had never felt like that before.

The smell of her own room refreshes her once she arrives home and enters her room. It's the first time she has felt anything like this. That her room has its own distinct odour. She notices every detail—the bookshelf, the record shelf—everything seems different today. As if she had resurrected with a new perspective—a different perspective that is causing her to see everything in a way she has never seen before.

She texts Olivia that she has arrived home. She falls deep asleep as soon as she lays down on her bed because she is exhausted. She falls into a deep sleep. She has a strange dream. In that dream, she appears to be a cat. It feels to her that her body has been transformed into a little cat from a human. And in front of her, there's another cat. Even though it's strange to be a cat all of a sudden, even in a dream, it appears that she's not worried or shocked about it. Instead, looking at the cat in front of her brings up a strange, peaceful feeling. And when she wakes up, the feeling lasts. Not even for a moment does she think that it was a strange dream. Instead, she feels like she wants to dream the same dream again when she falls asleep the next time.

"How did it go?" asks Kevin, entering her room after knocking as she was absorbed in reading after lunch. He's probably returning from a game or something, as it appears his body is sweaty and he seems tired. He takes a seat at the table as soon as he asks the question.

"Not bad at all." She replies with a smile. "It was totally different from what I thought. Honestly, I wasn't sure at the last moment. But it was worthy. A lot happened. I met a lot of nice people, you know."

"Sounds good enough. I kinda got worried last night for some reason." He says it in a serious tone.

Veronica wasn't expecting something like this from her brother. He has always been sarcastic about everything. She never saw him worried, and he never sounded worried to her. It's unusual for someone like him to say something like that. Maybe it's the same for all sarcastic people. We think they are funny and always happy, but inside, there are untold things that they barely express.

"Since when did you start to get worried about someone?"

"I don't know. He pauses and says, "Good that you're back. I need a shower now. Tell me later about who you met." He says this and heads out of the room.

She tells Kevin about everything that has happened to her later that night. How she got there and how she spent the night in a motel. How there was an old-fashioned café with jazz music playing all the time. What happened when she met Olivia and others. She just skips over the part about her romantic interest and how she's currently in a relationship. For a brief moment, she believes she can tell Kevin. Despite his young age, he was mature enough to understand her. Nonetheless, she decides to keep it a secret. He pays close attention to everything. This is also the first time she has seen her brother genuinely interested in something about her life. They've had conversations before, but not like this. Perhaps it was because she was so far away for the first time that he began to miss her. Perhaps people only realise the worth of another person when they are separated from them.

At night, her laptop screen pops up with a notification that Olivia is videocalling her. She takes a few seconds to adjust her hair and sitting position, then picks up the call.

"Hey!" says Olivia from the other end, her hands waving.

"Hey! What's up?"

"I'm alright. How was your trip? Any inconvinience?"

"No. It was okay. I didn't stop anywhere in between. I just drove all the time."

"You didn't eat? It was a long time."

"Yeah, I did. I did eat. I had food cans with me that I bought from a convenience store."

"How's everyone at home?"

"They seem to be okay. I just talked with my brother. I

told everything about the trip and all, you know."

"Everything?"

"Well I mean everything except our relationship."

From both ends, a faint laugh escapes. Because of the internet connection, the video lags for a while. After that, it returns.

"Is it okay now? Can you hear me?" Olivia speaks.

"Yeah, loud and clear."

"You know there's a Japanese proverb that says, *'koi to seki to wa kakusarenu'* which means, *'Love and a cough cannot be hidden'*."

"What does that mean? What does it have to do with coughing?

"Well, let's say you have a cough all of a sudden. You can't hold it inside for long, can you?"

"I don't know. Maybe I can try."

"You can try, but sooner or later you have to reveal it. And people will know that you're sick. So it says that love is just like that. You just have to let everyone know sooner or later."

The time on the clock continues to advance. But time is irrelevant in this case. Their conversation continues. Veronica believes she can speak for as long and as much as she wants. A euphoric feeling grips her like a bee on a flower in the spring.

Her world changes dramatically, an emotional metamorphosis that colours her days with new hues of significance. The monotony that once weighed her down has lifted, and even the dullest moments now have a glimmer of radiance. Her fingers dance over her phone, creating messages that are more than just words; they carry a piece of her heart to Olivia across the digital chasm. Her heart, once hidden beneath routine, now beats with a newfound fervour. She realises, like the first light of dawn, that she has fallen in love. A simple smile becomes the reflection of her joy, an expression that dances across her lips more frequently than before. Even when she is alone, her mind is racing with Olivia-related thoughts, like a treasured secret that only she has. A mirror develops into more than just a reflective surface; it develops into a gateway to self-awareness. More frequently, She notices Olivia's reflection in her own eyes. She views herself differently, as if Olivia's presence has revealed layers of her own beauty that she had never noticed before. She starts treating herself with reverence as a way of reflecting the concern she sees in Olivia's words and deeds. Love, like a delicate brushstroke, paints her days in vibrant colours of emotion. Her heart beats in sync with another person, a bond that transcends distance and time. The ordinary becomes extraordinary, and every step she takes is now a journey towards the person who has become the centre of her world for her.

The days begin to fly by. Spring has arrived. And with spring comes new life colours. The attachment grows stronger. The shy and introverted girl who struggled to make a small decision or have a small conversation with someone has changed. She is happier and more active than she has ever been. Perhaps this is how it always is when one is in love. She frequently wonders if this is true for everyone else or just her. Has the strict middle school teacher ever felt this way? Did she ever fall in love with or have feelings for someone? Did she ever smile when she was thinking of someone else? Did she ever love someone more than she loved being rude to students? How can someone be rude and in love at the same time? Or consider the student who used to bully almost everyone in class. Has he ever had the same thought? Did a subtle shift in feelings as lovely as cherry blossoms ever appear in his heart? Not just him, but the dictator who just threw a bomb at innocent children, the Mexican drug lord who just killed several people, the religious leader who just spread hatred against other religions in front of his followers, the abusive and irresponsible parents who left their child rot alone in a room, the lawyer who just sided with a murderer for money, the CEO who just yelled at her employees for no reason, the soldier who looks into his enemy's eye with hatred, not knowing what he's fighting for, have they ever fallen in love? Do they know how beautiful it is to make a promise to someone that you are almost certain of fulfilling? Do they know how it feels to look into someone's eyes and see themselves in the reflection? Perhaps they don't. How could they ever do what they are doing if they ever knew?

CHAPTER TEN

Despair

Everything is going swimmingly. Veronica's newfound self-assurance in life made her optimistic. She begins to try new things, such as eating out with her family for the first time. When the family used to go out to dinner, she never went because she thought it was just another boring thing to do. But she no longer skips it. She has also maintained contact with Catherine and even paid her a visit. She's been hanging out with her and other girls lately. They have also made plans for this weekend to see a film. It's strange to think about how she was a year ago and how she is now. She even applied to New York University. She is confident that her grades are sufficient to gain admission. A decision that was too difficult for her to make has now become a simple matter. She almost feels like a different person. And there is only one person responsible for this shift. There is only one person who has taught her the various perspectives on life. She's the one who made her believe in herself again. The rush of blood in her veins now feels like she can even stand up on a stage and give a speech about anything. Perhaps all a person needs in life is someone who can see them for who they are. Every person needs something or someone to cling to in life. And she has found someone that she can cling to.

Veronica enters the frenzy of Catherine's birthday party. The atmosphere is filled with laughter and lively conversations. Twinkling fairy lights cast a soft glow, illuminating the guests' animated expressions. Glasses clink in unison in toasts to the occasion and the commonality that binds everyone together. The flavour of delicious food tempts the senses, stimulating excitement and filling the space with a tantalising scent. Bodies sway to the music's rhythm, an irresistible beat that entices even the most hesitant dancers to join in. Laughter bursts forth like fireworks. Her gaze moves from person to person, taking in the spectacle of human connection and shared joy. Friends gather in pockets of joy, recounting anecdotes and exchanging laughs, while the birthday girl herself radiates pure happiness at the centre of it all.

Once she separates herself from others in a corner of the

room near the window with a drink in her hand, she checks her phone again and again to see the most anticipated text that she's been waiting to see since this afternoon. They have texted a lot and connected on video calls with each other, as that is the only option they have now to stay in touch. But lately, the schedule has been a little bit busy for Olvia. But still, it's been a long time since she hasn't replied, which becomes a concern for her at this moment. Every time she went off for a long time, she either said goodbye or goodnight because she was going to sleep. But this time it wasn't like that. Last time she texted, they were talking about a book by Sally Rooney.

A man approaches her while she is preoccupied with intrusive, mostly negative thoughts. Based on his appearance, she believes he, just like her, is feeling isolated. That could be the reason he approached her. Most people try to find someone who is similar to them. Because it makes them feel safer to know that they are not alone with their feelings. The man is tall and has a mullet haircut, but his hair is not as long in the back as a traditional mullet. However, this makes him appear appealing. Even in a large crowd, his sharp-chinned face is likely to be recognised.

"Are you alright?" he asks.

"Yeah, I'm fine. It's just a little crazy around here for me."

"I understand. I have similar feelings at times. I'm going for a smoke; would you like to join me?"

They are smoking outside, leaning against the wall. Momentarily, car horns can be heard. Both are smoking in silence without uttering a single word. A cat appears in front of them all of a sudden. He gets down and pats the cat.

"Do you like cats?" she asks while he is still busy patting the cat's back.

"Who doesn't like cats?" he asks back.

"I don't know, maybe those who have allergies to cats?"

"Haven't met anyone like that yet. Are you one of them?"

"No, not at all. I like cats too."

"Cats were a godlike creature in Ancient Egypt."

"I heard about that but I don't know much."

"Cats were tied to something more divine. The ancient Egyptians believed that cats would keep away bad spirits, and protect their companions from other threats such as dangerous snakes." He pauses and inhales a smoke while the cat he was patting moves and walks away from them. He continues standing up, "Killing a cat was illegal, but many pharaohs and other royalty were known to have their cats killed in the event of their own death so that their beloved pets could accompany them in the afterlife."

"Sounds bizarre to me."

"Most of the ancient history sounds bizarre if you think about it."

"Do you know anything about Japanese ancient history about cats?" she asks, taking a glance at him.

"As far as I know, Japanese people also believe cats are good luck. According to Japanese legend, once there was a storm going on while he came across a tree, and he saw a cat waving her paw towards the man. The man walks towards the cat, and right at that moment, a bolt of llightning strikes the place where the man was standing before. So, he thought he was lucky, and the cat brought the good luck to him by indicating waving its paw."

"That sounds more realistic than the other ones."

She wanted to tell him about the dream that she had where she was a cat, but she didn't. Later, she got to know that his name was Paul. He left his number for her, although she's quite certain that she will not call him ever. She will probably never see him again. But it seems like the man has an obsession with cats and ancient history.

Veronica walks down the familiar path home, her orange converse glowing like molten gold in the warm lamplight. Her steps have an almost rhythmic pace, reflecting the thoughts that run through her mind. She clutches her phone, her thumb intermittently swiping down the screen. Nonetheless, the screen remains defiantly devoid of any new messages. A troubling sensation arises within her chest, with roots of uncertainty winding their way through her thoughts. Her gaze flits between the illuminated screen and the dimly lit surroundings. A surge of insecurity tightens its grip, causing her pace to stutter for a moment. The possibility of an unanticipated event invades her thoughts, each second amplifying the silence emanating from her phone. She struggles with her thoughts, colliding with the strange sensation of vulnerability.

The solitude of the night seems to mirror her internal landscape. Doubt casts shadows on the outskirts of her mind. She thinks about the phone, wondering if she missed a call or a message, or if Olivia tried to reach her and ran into an unexpected obstacle. Her heart yearns for a response, for reassurance to calm her growing fears. In the context of her concerns, the lack of communication feels like an eternity. The silence becomes a moving picture.

She texted her several times, called several times wanting to know if everything was okay on the other end, but she received no response. Her terror grows stronger. She can't sleep unless she receives at least one text message. It's strange to consider how vulnerable you are when you're separated from someone. It's so easy to be unaware of what the person on the other end is going through.

She falls asleep right before sunrise after being awake most of the night. She has another dream, similar to the last one, in which she transforms into a cat, but this time it is slightly different. The other cat who appeared in her dream the last time and made her feel better does not appear this time. When she entered that dream, it felt so real to her that she almost didn't realise she was dreaming. So she started looking for the other cat, and when she couldn't find it, it made her sad. Also, this time, the dream lasts longer than the previous one. So she puts more effort into trying to find the other cat. But no matter how much she tries, it almost feels like she's just running around in a circle. No matter where she goes, she comes back to the same place. At one stage, she gives up, and right after that, she awakes from sleep.

When she wakes up, she checks her phone, but there is no text from the other end, which makes her feel even worse. She calls several times, but no one answers the phone. The more time passes, the more concerned she becomes. There is no way she would just ignore her like this out of nowhere.

This is also a new emotion for her. It's strange how a single moment of uncertainty and disconnection can cause a person's heart to erupt from the core, revealing how attached one was to that specific person. Kevin notices her concern. He inquires as to what transpired. She doesn't feel like telling him at first, but she eventually does. Everything that has happened since the beginning and how she fell for her. Kevin doesn't seem surprised at all. He appears to be calm and attentive to everything. He tries to persuade her that there might be a problem with her phone, that it was stolen, or that she lost it. But nothing seems to make her content.

The afternoon sky undergoes a transformation as clouds gather, obscuring the once-clear expanse. Raindrops, heavy and unrelenting, use liquid strokes of brush to paint the town. The percussion of rain on various surfaces resonates. She looks out at the drenched landscape, her thoughts mirroring the pouring rain. The outside world, covered in the gloomy wrap of the storm, reflects her inner turmoil. The familiarity she once had with rainy days, and the sense of renewal they brought, has been obscured by an inexplicable sense of uneasiness. This time, it's not the enchantment of the freshness or the gentle rhythm that draws her in. Instead, the turmoil in the storm reflects her internal conflict. The rain, which normally cleanses, now appears to stain her perceptions. The world, which often appeared revitalised and at ease after a shower, now appears to be entangled in a disheartening tangle.

The clock in her room keeps ticking, its steady sound breaking the silence. The top row of her bookshelf is half empty. Her phone sits atop the table. The familiar ringing signals the arrival of the moment, and she rushes to the table, her heart racing. Her gaze is drawn to the screen, the name of the person she is looking for illuminating her hopes. She quickly retrieves the phone and places it to her ear, full of hope. However, the voice on the other end carries an unexpected weight, tingeing her optimism with unease. The voice belongs to Finn, a startling twist that sends a shiver up her spine.

"Veronica?" Finn speaks with a cracked tone.

"Yeah? Where's Olivia? Why are you speaking Finn?" she replies fast.

Finn remains silent for a while. None of them speaks.

"Olivia had an accident yesterday." He finally reveals, his voice heavy with the gravity of the words. The utterance seems to cost him a great deal.

"What do you mean? Is she at the hospital? Tell me!" Her

voice with desperation, urgency in every word.

Another pause stretches, the silence palpable from his end.

"Tell me, damn it! Where is she? Why won't you talk?" Her words come with a mixture of fear and frustration.

And then, the truth strikes like a thunderbolt.

"She's no longer with us."

She is driving at a higher speed for the first time ever. She only cares that she gets to her destination; she doesn't care what happens. Her heart is completely torn apart by the news. When she learned about the death, it took her some time for her mind to fully process the situation. She had the feeling that she needed to cry but that she was unable to do so because something inside of her had become a heavy stone. There is currently no way to move that large stone. However, after a few hours of driving, something inside of her may have been able to temporarily move the stone. She bursts into tears while in the driver's seat. She is aware of what she has lost, and at this moment, nothing in the world could comfort her. She knows she has fallen from the sky like rain. And there is no other ground on which to fall further. She wipes away her tears and gets back behind the wheel.

She lacked anything suitable to wear to a funeral. She

didn't bring anything with her because she was rushing and in a hurry. She therefore wore a black suit that Finn gave her and that was the perfect size for her. She would give up her life if she could save Olivia. But she is aware that nothing could bring her back. She couldn't feel the way she did for anything.

The chairs are arranged in rows, their faces stricken with sadness as they huddle in little groups. She is drawn to an image of Olivia because it shows a moment in time that has since seemed to be frozen. Her mind is far from other people's words, so she only hears the faint echoes of their whispered conversations. Death is unavoidable, and even in the presence of others, she feels an isolated ache that only she understands. She lingers, unable to tear herself away from the casket that contains Olivia's physical vessel. As the procession begins to move, she finds herself trailing behind, as if a part of her still believes this is all a nightmare. But reality is unyielding, and she watches as she is lowered into the ground, taking a piece of her heart with her. She wishes to hold her just like the ground will hold her coffin till the end of time.

In the aftermath, she stands alone at the grave as people scatter and the world resumes its pace. Finn follows her. He can't seem to look her in the eyes. He feels guilty about not informing her sooner because he lacked the courage to do so. There are millions of choices available, but at the end of the day, a person should only make decisions that they will not regret.

After that, they sit quietly beside the lake on a promenade. Nobody has yet broken the silence. Their heavy hearts are reflected on their faces, making them appear as if they have never learned to smile.

"I'm truly sorry." Finn finally speaks up.

Veronica maintains her own silence. She is deafeningly quiet.

"Sorry for not informing you earlier." Finn continues.

This time, she looks at him with a blank expression but doesn't say anything. She pulls a smoke pack from her pocket. She takes one out for her and then hands one to him. Today, it seems as though the wind is also grieving for the loss because there isn't much of it blowing. They used a lighter to light their smoke without covering it with their hands because there was no wind to make it struggle.

"You know, she told me about you a few days ago. About you two being in love. I kind of sensed that before too, but this was the first time I'd heard of it from her. She really liked you. She was happy. When you were here, she seemed to be so happy too."

A few metres away from them, a pigeon appears, resting its wings on the ground. Their eyes both turn to it. It remains motionless for a short while. Then it begins to move forward. A few seconds later, it takes off in flight.

"I know you're angry with me. You have every right to be. But I didn't know what to do. Michelle wasn't there either. If she was there, she could have let you know earlier."

"I'm not angry with you." Veronica finally speaks. "Even if I knew earlier, it wouldn't be able to save her." Her voice sounds empty.

A jet ski strolls by on the lake at full speed. The woman riding it seems happy. It's strange to think how under the same sky and in a short distance, someone is mourning and someone is having the time of their life.

She can still clearly recall how she felt when her grandma passed away. Death is a natural occurrence. Nobody's life will last for ever. On the other hand, the idea of immortality and eternal life is absurd. In the event that you are the only person left, could living forever really be fulfilling? Is perpetual happiness satisfying if it blinds you to the complexity of life? She is perplexed by everything. But nothing she says to her can justify or make it easier for her to accept the death of the person she has just experienced.

CHAPTER ELEVEN

Change

NYU's acceptance letter arrives. Her parents' happiness is palpable, and their smiles are brighter than ever. Her expression, however, remains unchanged. Her heart does not respond in kind as her parents congratulate her and express their pride. Her emotions are still anchored by the weight of her recent loss. The news that used to light up her world with possibilities now feels muffled. The smile that should have been on her lips feels distant, enigmatic. The contrast between their joy and her quiet sorrow is heartbreaking.

Kevin's efforts to reach her are met with a deafening silence. Veronica remains hidden in her grief, despite his best intentions and genuine concern. Kevin's efforts are not unappreciated by her. In fact, she appreciates his presence and unwavering support. But the enormity of her loss has rendered her speechless. Every attempt at conversation feels like an impossible task, as if she's standing on the brink of an abyss with no words to bridge the gap. Long pauses and distant gazes punctuate her interactions with Kevin. She hears and sees his concern, but her own voice is silenced, buried beneath the weight of her grief. It's as if Olivia's absence has silenced not only her outward expressions but also the internal monologue that used to guide her interactions. Kevin's understanding personality does not push her, and she appreciates his patience. While she lacks the words to express her sorrow, she hopes he can see it in her eyes, in the way she carries herself, and in the gloom that has settled over her like a shroud.

Perhaps, in time, she'll find the courage to express her feelings to him. But, for the time being, her silence speaks volumes. And as Kevin remains by her side, she finds comfort in the presence of someone who cares, even if she can't fully express what's on her mind.

Her father is so pleased with her admission to NYU that he offers to buy her a new car. But she refuses, saying that she would rather have a piano instead.

It's an April afternoon. Veronica is standing outside the baseball field while smoking, where Kevin is playing. The pitcher, a strong high schooler with an age-defying physique, takes his stance on the mound. His muscular build and experienced arm lend him authority. He throws the ball with precision with each pitch, his heavy arm producing impressive speed. The first strike echoes through the air, the crack of the ball colliding with the gloves of the keeper. Kevin, unfazed by the early setback, prepares for the next delivery. He adjusts his grip, a small but deliberate movement. The pitcher winds up, unleashing the ball with commanding force. Kevin's gaze is fixed on the approaching sphere. The contact of the ball with the bat creates a loud sound that travels far beyond the field. The ball sails away outside the netting. And in between those moments, her brother runs from base to base and makes it a home run.

After the game, they sat side by side on the field, leaning against the netting. Kevin is enjoying a hotdog and coke brought to him by Veronica.

"Never thought you were gonna come to see me play someday." Speaks kevin.

"Just wanted to see how you play, before I leave for New York."

"When are you leaving?"

"This Friday."

"Hope you get a better life there, sis." He takes his time to gulp down the bite that he just took, and then he drinks the coke. "You know Shanon?"

"Who's Shanon?"

"The redhead girl from my class. I told you about her. You forgot already."

"When?"

"See, you're getting older. Now you have memory problems." He says it with a laugh.

Veronica tries to remember if she knows anyone named Shanon, but she can't.

"It's alright. Don't worry. There's no Shanon. I'm just messing with ya."

"What? That doesn't make any sense." Her voice still sounds empty even when she says anything surprising or exciting.

"It's something like when you have no knowledge about a certain thing or a person, no matter what I say is going to sound believable to you. Because that information space about that person or thing in your brain is empty. I can fill it up with anything."

"Since when did you get so philosophical?"

"Always, but you never saw it." He continues after a silence, "Are you going to tell me what happened or not?"

She opens up this time. She tells him about how Olivia died and how it made her feel. How she could do anything possible to get back the time that she spent with her. If there was one way to turn back time, she would do it.

"You know, I kinda wanna say that it's gonna get better, but I don't know if it will. I can only sense how you feel. But I do hope that it gets better for you. She would have wanted that. She won't probably like to see you this way. She would love to see you smile instead." He says this after listening to everything attentively.

The afternoon sun starts to go down on the horizon. It disappears slowly. An elderly woman walks by with her dog as they walk together towards home.

Life stops for some, but their memories are carried by those who remember. The pictures of Olivia that she took that autumn are displayed in frames on her table in her New York apartment. It's a busy city. She is engulfed by the sounds—a cacophony of honking horns, chatter, and footsteps that blend into a rhythm that defines the city's heartbeat. Skyscrapers reach for the sky, their reflective surfaces reflecting the lively energy below. Glass and steel mingle with stone and brick in a harmonious fusion of old and new. Yellow taxis weave their way through traffic. Pedestrians walk with purpose. Veronica finds herself navigating a maze of streets and avenues, each with its own distinct personality. Fifth Avenue, flanked by luxury boutiques and cultural landmarks, stretches with regal grace. With its neon lights and frenetic energy, Times Square pulsates. The peaceful expanse of Central Park provides a green oasis in the midst of the city's bustle. The Broadway theatres come alive in the evening with spectacular performances. The city is never quiet. Unlike people, it is never silent. People may go silent at times, but the city does not. Sometimes she thinks it's better for her to be surrounded by constant sounds that are louder than the sounds in her head. She has recently begun to listen to music at a higher volume. It distracts her from her thoughts for a while.

She loses herself when she looks in the mirror. She walks through the streets with a blank expression on her face. She cries on public transport while wearing headphones. But her tears aren't falling from her eyes. Her heart is the only thing that is crying. Her dreams are confusing to her. She no longer appears to be a cat. There is no longer a dream that makes her feel good when she wakes up. Instead, it wakes her up in the middle of the night. She has difficulty falling asleep at night. As a result, she spends most of her nights awake, writing in her diary or trying to concentrate on reading. She feels hollow inside, as if there is a hole.

It's a Sunday morning. She watches through her window as the sky is overcast, but it doesn't seem like it's going to rain. It's one of those clouds that makes you think it's going to rain heavily, but it actually won't. It looks gloomy, but the clouds are moving, and soon the sky will probably be clear. She sits on her piano and thinks for a while, closing her eyes. She touches the keys with her delicate hands and hits the opening notes of 'Colour Me Blue' by Akane. She plays the notes slower than in the original piece. She stops for a moment, then starts playing again. This time, the notes match the timing of the original piece. A gentle wind moves the closed curtain of the window.

It's around midnight when she feels a sudden urge to go out. Time is a fluid concept here, and the lines between night and day blur into a rolling continuum. She goes to a pub where an unknown musician is covering a song. Her fingers tenderly strum an acoustic guitar, weaving the intimate chords of Big Thief's 'Change' into the very fabric of the night, unaffected by the dim surroundings. Her hair seems like she had a buzzcut a month ago or two. Now the hair is growing, but it's still short. She's singing the song in a soothing voice. The whole pub is silent, listening to her perform as if she has drawn everyone in with a mesmerising atmosphere. The world recedes in this suspended moment, and she becomes a part of the shared experience that binds the audience together. The lyrics construct like a dialogue with the listener's soul, as if the performer and audience members are having a private discussion.

The room erupts in applause as the song's final notes are played. A gentle smile appears on the singer's lips as she expresses gratitude to the audience. Her attention shifts as she feels the slight touch of someone's hand on her shoulder. She turns around and sees Paul. It doesn't take much time for her to remember him, even though they only had a single interaction before.

"Hey!" he says with a smily face.

"Hi."

"I'm surprised to see you."

"Why?" she asks.

"What do you mean, why? I didn't know you were in New York. Wait, do you remember me?"

"Yes."

"Really?"

"Yeah, you're Paul."

"So you do remember me. Aren't you surprised to see me?"

"No."

"Did I tell you I live in New York?"

"I don't think you did."

Paul seems like a nice guy to her just to talk to. Even though she doesn't have much to say, she doesn't seem bothered by some company. Paul invites her to join him for a drink, and she accepts. They sit across from each other, mostly in silence. Paul doesn't seem to mind the silence either. It appears that he is still at ease with the interaction. Even though her responses were brief, one would assume she was uninterested if she spoke to someone in that manner. After taking a sip from the glass, they make eye contact. Paul has pierced his left ear, she notices. His hairstyle remained the same. Buzzed on the side but kept the front and back medium. He's wearing a plain blue T-shirt.

"So what are you doing in New York?" Paul asks.

"I'm studying at NYU.

"That's cool." He turns his head to the left and waves his arms at some guy standing there as they make eye contact. It seems like they knew each other. He looks back at Veronica and continues, "So what are you studying?"

"English Literature."

He gives an expression as he's kinda impressed and says, "That's even cooler."

Veronica is deafeningly quiet. She's at a loss for words. She isn't in the mood to say anything either. But for some reason, having Paul in front of her sort of makes her feel slightly better. She would have felt awkward if this were her one-year-ago self. But she's no longer awkward at all.

"You know I'm not much of a literature guy. But I do read sometimes."

"What do you do?" She finally asks.

"Like work?"

"Yeah."

"I work part time, actually. I go to NYU too. Institute of Fine Arts."

"I thought you didn't go to school."

"Why did you think that? Do I look too old?"

"No, I just thought. How old are you anyway?"

"How old do I look?"

"I don't know. Twenty?"

"I'll take that as a compliment that you think I'm younger than my age. I'm twenty-one."

The guy who waved towards Paul a few minutes ago approaches the table and shakes hands with Paul as he stands up. They share gestures, and the guy asks if he's going to come tomorrow to his party. Paul says he's going to try his best, but he has something to do tomorrow. Paul doesn't introduce Veronica to him. The guy doesn't pay much attention to her either. He says goodbye to Paul after that short interaction.

Paul sits back on his table, grabs his drink, and says, "Sorry, that was a friend."

"It's alright."

"Do you wanna go for a walk?" He proposes.

"I won't mind. But there's something you should know. I'm a lesbian, and you don't have any chance with me, in case you're wondering."

His reaction seems more normal than she thought he would be, but still, with a calm voice, he speaks. "I kinda guessed that."

"How?"

"How what?"

"How did you guess that?"

"The way you guessed that I didn't go to college. Besides, don't worry; there's a lot more between a man and a woman than sex."

They left the pub and started walking. Paul seems like a nice guy to her. There's something about his way of speaking that comforts her. He speaks in a calm manner. It's almost as if there's no rush for anything.

The streets aren't quiet like her neighbourhood. Neon signs illuminate the night, advertising theatres and enticing passersby to discover the city's entertainment options. Delivery trucks double-park, their drivers rushing to unload goods as soon as possible, to ensure the city never sleeps.

They are walking silently. Even though the surroundings are noisy, the silence among them is noticeable. But it doesn't make either of them uncomfortable. Veronica believes it is beneficial to meet someone who is both quiet and not awkward. Unspoken silence makes most people nervous. Sometimes it's necessary to be able to sit or walk in silence with someone. Finally, Paul interrupts the silence when they come near the promenade of the riverside park. They stand leaning against the promenade as they talk.

"Do you ever wonder how life would be if people worked at night and slept during the day?" he asks randomly.

"No. It's strange to think that." She replies.

"I know. That's why I wonder how it would be. How many people are asleep right now, you think?"

"That's a strange question. How would I know the number?"

"No, I meant in general, like how many in percentage?"

"I think less than fifty percent. I see more people out at night than day here."

"An average human spends nearly half of their life sleeping." I think it's better to be awake once in a while rather than miss what's happening around." Paul remarks.

Paul turns around and faces the river, putting his elbows on the promenade. Veronica asks if he has a ciggarette. Without saying anything, Paul reaches into his pocket, pulls out a pack of cigarettes, and deftly extracts two. He hands one to her, their fingers briefly brushing, and then he lit the tip of her cigarette with his lighter.

After lighting his own, he asks Veronica, "Don't you ever smile?"

"Maybe I don't. Why? Are you bored already?"

"Quiet this opposite. It feels mysterious to me to think that I've met someone who I've never seen smiling."

A couple passes in front of them as they go silent once again.

"You ever lost someone, Paul? Like a friend, family, or someone close?"

"Not yet. Why?"

She takes a long drag of her cigarette and then says, "I have. Do you want to know how it feels?"

"Go on."

"At first, when you get the news, your body feels numb. It almost feels like you can't feel anything. You can't react to anything at first. It's like someone has injected you with anaesthesia, and now you don't feel a thing. Then slowly, the sensation comes back. And you start to feel. Now you're aware of what just happened, and you start to feel bad. You feel blue. You realise the loss. Time passes, and the pain becomes sharper. You might say people move on as time passes, but I don't think that's the case for everyone. The memories haunt you. It gives you a bittersweet feeling. But it haunts you. Your dreams start to change. And at last, everything makes you empty inside, like you're just hollow."

"Who have you lost?"

"Someone I've loved."

For a moment Paul finds himself a bit lost in thoughts. He doesn't immidietly say something. He finds it difficult to react to that. He tries to come up with something, and when he finally does, he says, "How do you think your life would have turned out if you never met her?"

"You're asking if I'd be better off without her?"

"No, not like that. I mean, just a thought, a different view."

"I don't know how it would have been. But I don't think I regret any moment I shared with her."

"See, that's what I was talking about. It's better this way that it happened. If it had never happened and you had never met her, you wouldn't have had the moments you shared with her. Moments are precious. Memories are meant to be remembered." he explains.

"I get it. But isn't it strange to realise that one day you're spending time with someone, then the next day that person becomes a memory? And you know those moments will never repeat themselves. The person will never talk to you again. And life was good before that person died. But the death has changed everything. The world is still going at its own pace. The only difference is that the person is not here anymore. They are just a memory inside your head." She states.

"I don't think I can feel that because I've never lost someone yet. You can't feel something until it happens to you. But I understand your point. The grief that you're going through is probably intolerable. I could say it's going to get better, but I don't know that either. I can just hope that it does get better."

"Thanks for being honest Paul." She mutters. "Do you have someone you like?"

"What do you think?"

"I don't think you do, because if you had, you wouldn't have approached me."

"I think you're right. But I don't mind that. I mean, maybe

I just haven't found the right person yet. I can wait."

When she speaks with Paul, she feels a strong sense of security, which encourages her to open up and share her thoughts. Although they aren't particularly close, there is a positive connection between them that gives her hope. She's allowing herself to be vulnerable for the first time in a long time, and it's a relief to know that at least one person understands her. She continues to talk about her journey and the events that led her to this point. Paul pays close attention, asking thoughtful questions and making supportive comments.

CHAPTER TWELVE

Evening Sky

Veronica finds herself on the rooftop of a tall building, surrounded by darkness. As she scans her surroundings, her gaze is drawn to Olivia, who is perched perilously on the safety railing. Olivia's laughter fills the room, but she is unaware of Veronica's presence. Her gaze is fixed on something distant as she moves, almost dancing on the railing's edge, oblivious to the danger. Her heartbeat quickens, and a sense of urgency drives her forward as she rushes towards Olivia, fearful of the imminent threat. But just as she's about to reach her, she wakes up, realising it was all a vivid and unsettling dream that had transported her to a world of fear and concern.

Veronica's gaze is drawn to the clock in the bottom right corner of her phone screen, which reads 3:11 a.m. The room wraps her in silence and darkness, but she is restless. She sighs, a slight sheen of sweat forming on her brow. As she pushes herself up, her hand braces against the bed. She throws her blanket aside, swings her legs out of bed, and steps onto the cold floor. She splashes water on her face in front of the bathroom mirror, the coolness giving her a brief moment of clarity. As she studies her reflection, the dark circles under her eyes become more visible, and her dishevelled hair adds to the image of anxiety. She slips into a comfortable tracksuit, the fabric snugly hugging her body. Then she steps out into the quiet night with her headphones over her ears.

As she runs through the streets, the sidewalks stretch out mostly empty in front of her. She ignores the closed stores, quiet pubs, and gates along her path, her gaze fixed firmly on the path ahead. The rhythm of her run was a steady beat in the early morning silence. She continues her run through the park, circling its easy paths. She recognises the need for a brief break after a long stretch of straight-ahead running to keep her body cool. She slows her pace and takes a breather.

Her gaze turns to a cat resting peacefully on a bench nestled beneath a tree a few metres away. She approaches the cat, thinking it must be sleeping. As she gets closer and comes around to the front, she notices that the cat is wide awake, its bright, attentive eyes locked on her with a curious expression. She takes a seat beside the quiet cat, who is unaffected by her presence. She slowly extends her hands and begins to pat the cat gently; her touch is met with a feeling of calm that seems to surround them both. Veronica carefully lifts the pleased cat onto her lap, gently cradling it. Her hands continue to stroke the cat's back in a soothing rhythm, and the cat's eyes narrow, indicating how much comfort it now finds in her company. She tenderly lifts the silent cat, gently cradling it in her arms. The cat is deafeningly silent, not uttering a single meow. She decides to take the cat home with her.

She gently places the cat on the floor when she arrives at her flat. The curious animal begins to move around the room, exploring its new surroundings. She takes off her shoes, goes to the refrigerator, and pulls out a bottle of milk. She pours some into a small bowl and places it on the floor. The cat approaches eagerly, drawn by the scent of the milk, and begins to slurp it up. She sits down on the floor and stares at the cat for a while.

As the sun rises through her window, its gentle rays first kiss the glass, creating a fleeting reflection on her room's floor. Her attention is drawn to this play of light after a refreshing shower. She walks up to the window and opens it slowly and deliberately. The sun's warm embrace pours into the room, surrounding her in a radiant glow. She lets the towel that had been cloaking her fall to the floor, exposing her skin to the sun's caress. She closes her eyes and surrenders to the comforting warmth, savouring the sensation as it washes over her.

Her black boots create a rhythmic sound with every step she takes, echoing through the bustling streets as she passes by a street of unfamiliar faces. Each person she encounters is a mere passerby in her own narrative, moving towards their respective destinations while she navigates her own path with a gaze fixed ahead. Her eyes occasionally dip down but rarely make contact with the eyes of those she passes. At her campus, she finds herself in a quiet corner, where she sits in solitude, eating her breakfast with little regard for her surroundings. The once-observant eyes that used to wander and take in the world around her have grown distant, now focused solely on her own inner thoughts and journey. The lecture hall has no influence on her interest. She sits in her seat, her gaze fixed in a direction that shifts from time to time, but her thoughts appear to be far removed from the class. The laughter and chatter of her classmates come to her like distant echoes.

She takes the subway to get back to her place. The subway is crowded as always. Her headphones suppress the usual cacophony of tube station sounds, from the clattering of wheels on tracks to the murmur of conversations. She waits for her train on the platform, patient and composed.

When the train arrives, she and the other passengers board. She sits in an empty seat; a few seconds later, an elderly woman appears and sits beside her, holding a large bag. A young couple takes their seat across from her. The girl closes her eyes and falls asleep on the boy's shoulder a few minutes after the train begins to move. He notices this and maintains his position so that she is not bothered. Veronica looks at them for a moment before returning her attention to her phone.

She visits a nearby store to buy cat food for her recently adopted cat. The cat approaches her as she enters her room with the bag of cat food in her hand and lets out a meow, a first-time vocalisation. Veronica quickly opens the packet and pours some cat food into a dish for the hungry cat. She pauses to stroke the cat's head. She finally returns to her bed after ensuring the cat is eating contentedly, releasing the tension in her body as she sinks into its comfort, ready to relax after a day filled with moments of solitude.

She places some previously cooked noodles on a plate and microwaves them. She observes the plate slowly rotating inside the microwave as it warms.

She sits at her table, fork in hand, staring at the plate of noodles in front of her. But then a flood of overwhelming emotion runs through her. After a few seconds, she bursts into tears, her whimpering sobs filling the room. For a while, she just let her tears flow, the weight of her emotions too much for her to bear at the time. She is aware that she has reached rock bottom in her life. Loneliness has engulfed her like a goldfish in a bowl. She can no longer swim outside the bowl.

Her voice is still heavy as she calls Paul. She's at a loss for what to do. She doesn't even know anyone in this town. So Paul was the only person she could reach at the time.

She doesn't waste any time when Paul arrives at her door. She rushes over to him, wrapping her arms around him and burying her tear-streaked face in his chest, her sobs wracking her body. The agonising expression of pain lasts several minutes, her emotions spilling out in the safety of his presence. Paul remains silent, his face calm. He cradles her in his arms, offering her the comfort of his presence as she lets out the pent-up pain and sorrow.

They are both sitting in her apartment building's dimly lit corridor. Paul leans against the wall, facing Veronica. With a thoughtful expression, she starts the conversation.

"I had a dream of her last night."

"What was it?" Paul asks, his voice still gentle and calm.

"I saw her dancing. On a rooftop. She was smiling and dancing. She seemed happy. When I tried to reach her, I woke up."

"Maybe it's a message from her. She's trying to tell you that wherever she is, she's happy."

"Do you believe in the afterlife, Paul?"

Paul thinks for a moment before responding, "I don't know about that. But I believe there might be something that is unknown to us."

For a while, silence comes in between them. Paul then continues,

"You know, in traditional Japanese belief, people believe that when a person dies, their soul lives on the planet of the dead. According to them, the dead are always nearby, their spirits wandering around in mountains, woods, and other places, and they may even visit their loved ones once in a while. Some believe they visit in dreams."

"Do you think it's true?"

"It could be. I can't say it's true. But I don't have anything to say that it's completely false."

"Do you think she sees us?"

"She might be. Who knows, maybe she's present in this room right now."

A faint smile arrives on both of their lips as he says that.

"If I die, will I be able to join her on the planet of the dead?"

"No."

"Why?"

"I didn't tell you this, but there's also division on the planet of the dead. Just like different countries on the planet of the living. So, you can be on another side of the planet of the dead, which can be the opposite of her. Maybe you will forget her memories too if you do so."

"I wanna kill myself."

"I'm sure she wouldn't have wanted that."

"You know, I once met a weird guy while I was driving through the woods. He wanted a lift, so I gave him one. I drove him a few kilometres. He seemed empty and totally at a loss. I felt bad for him. I don't even know if he's still alive or not. Today, I realised my life is slowly becoming like his. Now, I talk the same way he used to talk. My face kinda looks the same as his face."

"You can always find yourself again."

"I don't know if I'll ever be able to do that."

"Don't you think it's gonna be a waste not to see the potential that you will become someday? I know it's hard, but you will get through it, I believe. Life is like that sometimes. But you shouldn't give up this early. Live for her. So that you can remember her. Remember the good memories that you've had."

The cat is approaches towards them. It comes to a halt in front of Paul and meows softly, pleading for his attention. Paul reaches out, scoops the cat into his arms, and gently places the cat on his lap.Paul begins to pat the cat's back with a soothing touch. The air is filled with the cat's contented purring.

"I didn't know you had a cat."

"I didn't have him until this morning."

Paul raises an eyebrow. "You adopted a cat this morning?"

She nodds. "Yeah. Saw him resting on the park bench and just took him."

Paul grins. "Well, that's good. You have a new friend now to take care of."

"Seems like it."

"What have you named him?"

"I don't know; I haven't decided yet. What do you think I

should name him?"

"I have no idea. I'm not good with names. Maybe, Jonas?"

A soft chuckle comes out of Veronica.

"Jonas? Who names a cat Jonas? I've never heard something like that."

Paul shrugs and says, "Told you I'm not good."

Their attention turns to the cat, who suddenly jumps from Paul's lap and saunters into the living room.

"Paul?" she calls out, shifting her glance towards him.

"yeah?"

"What do you think is gonna happen to you in five years?"

"I don't know that. I don't think anyone knows what's gonna happen to them until it actually happens. But if you ask me where I want to see myself in five years, then I would probably say that I want to see myself living happily with a better job and financial stability. I don't have many big dreams and all."

The cat approaches them again, unfazed by its previous encounters. This time, it's drawn to Veronica. She extends her fingers and gently strokes the cat's chin, her touch tender and soothing. As her fingers caress the cat's fur, the cat, who appears to appreciate her gentle gesture, sits beside her, its eyes narrowing in contentment.

"Do you wanna know how I see myself in five years?" She

asks Paul.

"How?"

"I don't know. Maybe in my grave."

Paul looks at her silently for a moment, and she looks back. Paul's lips slowly widen, as if he's about to smile, and he finally chuckles. Veronica finds herself smiling with his rhythm without intention or effort.

"What?" She asks.

"Nothing. You heard about that moral question where there are two ships and in one ship there are hundred passengers, and on the other ship there are like two hundred. Now, one ship will sink, but you can save only one ship from sinking. Now, most people would say they'll save the one with two hundred people; in that way, they are saving more people. So, my dad once said, How about I take those one hundred people on my ship and let the empty ship sink? In that way, I will be saving everyone. There's no condition in the question that I can't take them."

"Where's your dad now?"

"He had an accident two years ago. Since then he's been in a coma."

"I'm sorry for that."

Paul replies unexpectedly, "Don't be," he says gently. "I think he has lived a worthy life."

"What was his profession?"

"He was a police officer. Served for twenty long years. He used to tell me stories about his encounters when I was young."

"Do you remember any story that he told you?" She asks with curiousity this time.

"I do. A lot of." He responses.

She nodds eagerly. "Tell me one. One that interested you a lot."

For the first time since meeting her, Paul felt she was truly interested in something. She leaned in closer to hear his story. He told her a story about his father investigating a case of three people going missing while driving on a highway. Surprisingly, nothing was discovered about them. Then, a few days later, the same thing happened to another guy driving through the same area. His father had a colleague who was dead set on winning the case. She was determined to solve the mystery in any way she could. As a result, she used to expend extra effort searching for areas and items. Then, one night, while she was exploring the area by herself, she vanished. There's no way of knowing where they went or what happened to them right now. Nobody seems to be able to solve this mystery. Even their cars were nowhere to be found.

A glimpse of the morning sun gets into the room through the curtains. It falls right onto Veronica's face. She wakes up. Paul had stayed at her place last night. He's still sleeping on the couch in the living room. She gets to the kitchen and prepares breakfast for both of them. A few minutes later, Paul wakes up too. He asks her if he could use the shower. Veronica says to feel free about it. They sit at the dinner table together and have breakfast. Paul thanks her for the breakfast and everything. He offers to drive her to her class. She agrees.

Veronica enrolls in the modern literature course, guided by the knowledge of a lecturer named Anna Kartvelishvili, a Georgian woman with a deep love of literature. Anna had a remarkable ability to bring the pages of the books they studied to life, inviting her students to look beyond the text and into the artistic evolution of a fascinating era. Anna emphasises in her lectures that modern literature is more than just deciphering words on paper. It was a dynamic journey through an ever-changing artistic landscape, a reflection of the times' societal, cultural, and philosophical currents. She painted a vivid picture of how the very style of modern literature had evolved, changing shape with each passing decade. She enlightens the class with her observations, describing how literary innovations once erupted like fireworks of imagination, only to be absorbed into the fabric of the literary canon or, in some cases, metamorphosed into entirely new forms.

Veronica feels a different impulse today, so she skips the subway and instead waits at the bus stop. She sits down on a bench, looking down the road, waiting for her bus. An unexpected sight catches her attention as she lingers there. Anna, her lecturer from the previous class, has also arrived at the bus stop. However, the Anna she saw now was quite different from the composed and erudite figure she remembered from class. The lecturer's facial expression changed dramatically, as if a previously hidden aspect of her personality had been revealed outside of the confines of academia. While taking a class and explaining lectures to her students, she seems to be an extraordinary human with the extraordinary quality of seeking the attention of anyone and telling them the story that they all want to hear. But now, she seems like a very ordinary person waiting for the bus to reach her destination. Her face portrays sadness, which Veronica can observe from a distance. She doesn't know if anyone else can observe that, or if it's just her that notices the emotions of other human beings just by reading their facial expression. If it's really true, then she might as well have an extraordinary quality of reading emotions, she thinks.

Raindrops begin to fall from the sky unexpectedly, taking her by surprise. With no other option, she grabs her umbrella and unfurls it, taking shelter beneath its protective cover. A few metres away, her teacher, still without an umbrella, tries in vain to shield herself from the rain, raising her hands futilely above her head. Veronica, moved by her teacher's troubles, decides to intervene. She approaches her and offers some much-needed shade with a portion of her umbrella.

"Thanks." Says Anna.

She simply nods, as if to say that it was no problem at all.

Anna takes a cigarette from her pocket, but before lighting it, she gives Veronica a thoughtful look.

"Do you mind if I smoke?"

She shakes her head. "Not at all. Go ahead."

Anna nods appreciatively and then extends the pack towards her. "Would you like one?"

She considers it for a moment before accepting it with a polite nod. "Sure, thank you."

Anna lights hers up and then lights the one kept in Veronica's mouth.

She takes a contemplative drag from her cigarette and then speaks, exhaling a puff of smoke as she does so. "I'm attending your modern literature course this semester."

Anna raises an eyebrow, a flicker of recognition crossing her face. "Ah, I thought you looked familiar. Is it your first semester?"

"Yeah."

"I guessed that too. You look young."

The bus hasn't arrived yet, and the unexpected rain has temporarily slowed the busy flow of pedestrians. What had once been a filled thoroughfare is now sparsely populated. The rain has acted as a natural pause button, scattering only a few people across the otherwise deserted landscape, their presence marked by glistening wet pavement and the lingering scent of petrichor in the air.

"I like the rain." Anna says casually, her voice is filled with nostalgia.

"I hate the rain." Veronica responds almost instantly.

"Why?"

"I used to like it too. I liked the smell after the rain. But now, I don't."

"There must be a reason behind it."

"It reminds me of something that makes me sad."

"You do sound sad." As she speaks, she delicately taps her cigarette with a finger, allowing the burnt ashes to fall.

"Maybe."

"Do you write?"

"Write what?"

"Anything about your feelings."

"I used to write in my diary but I stopped recently."

Anna offers a thoughtful perspective, "You should write them down more often. Your thoughts, your sadness," she suggests. "It's the sad people who write the most beautiful poems. Most of the literature that we read, it comes out from grief and longing. People don't talk when they have so many things to tell. They write."

The bus arrives a few moments later, but it's not the one on her route. Anna, having finished her brief respite from the rain, boards the bus again, grateful for the shelter provided by the umbrella. She watches as the bus departs.

She stays there for a few minutes longer, alone with her thoughts, until her own bus arrives.

Veronica's first reaction upon entering her flat is to lift her cat with affection, greeting her new companion, who eagerly approaches her the moment she crosses the threshold. The cat responds with a joyful purr, content and comforted by its owner's warmth. She then feeds her cat, using the cat food from the packet she bought the day before.

She takes a cold shower, feeling the icy water flow over her body. She stands beneath the stream of water, allowing it to wash away the accumulated fatigue. She stands in peaceful silence, her eyes closed, embracing the invigorating sensation of the cold water gently coursing over her.

She proceeds to dry herself off after the cold shower, the soft towel absorbing the moisture from her skin. She looks down at her slightly longer hair as she wraps the towel around her body. She runs a towel through it, the damp strands brushing against her fingertips. The idea of cutting it short lingers in her mind, and it is something she will consider in the coming days.

She dresses herself up and plays a special playlist on her speaker. The one that Olivia made for her once. Every song on the playlist reminds her of the moments she spent with her. A sense of nostalgia touches her mind. The top row of her bookshelf, which was half empty when she was at home, is now full of new books. Her gaze moves to the window, her focus drawn to the weather outside. The rain has stopped completely, leaving behind a transformed sky painted with the enchanting hues of a yellowish evening glow. It's a distinct and soothing palette that only appears after a refreshing rain. She walks up to the window and stands there, looking up at the sky. The music from the playlist is still playing. She senses the gradual fading of the sun's presence as time passes, even though she cannot see the sun from here. The fading light and shifting tones in the sky are unmistakable indicators that the day is drawing to a close and darkness is approaching. But, she thinks, the sun will rise again after the night, brightening the day once more, and countless people will pass through the street, each with their own purpose for the day. The speaker plays the final verse of Alana Henderson's 'On Board' which reaches her ears,

> *"Don't forget, ships were not built to be safe*
>
> *And in all my life's mistakes*
>
> *You were not one*
>
> *'Cause all I've ever done*
>
> *All I've ever done*
>
> *Is love you*
>
> *To the bottom of the deep blue sea"*

Epilogue

The auditorium is packed with students and members of the reading community. Their chattering sounds have taken over the place. It's architecture is an example of modern aesthetics. Its clean lines and minimalist design exude elegance and sophistication. The walls, which are embellished with artistic panels, seamlessly integrate technology into the space. Paul can be seen sitting in the front row with a girl she met a year ago. They are now a couple. Her name is Jane. They both appear to be very happy, smiling and laughing with each other while conversing.

A tall blond man stands on stage, watching everything and making sure everything is in order. He is the event's host. He double-checks whether the mic is properly positioned on him. Then he draws everyone's attention with a gesture. Then he introduces the show's guest and tells everyone to greet her. With a smile on her face, the guest steps onto the stage. She appears to be dressed up in a black tuxedo. While she enters, the audience erupts in applause. She gives a gentle nod of appreciation to the audience. She shakes hands with the show's host before taking her seat. Her legs are crossed as she sits. She scans the audience for a second before coming to a halt in the front row, where Paul was seated. Paul gives her a friendly wave. She responds with a soft smile.

The auditorium, which was once alive with laughter and chatter, has now fallen silent. The host adjusts his sitting position to be more comfortable before asking the first question, "So, Ms. Veronica, where do you get your writing inspirations from?"

The End

Playlist

'Farewell' by Bob Dylan

'Both Sides Now' by Joni Mitchell

'Laura' by Charlie Parker

'Dream a Little Dream of Me' by Doris Day

'A Foggy Day' by Oscar Peterson

'Blue in Green' by Miles Davies

'Veronica' by Cornelis Vreeswijk

'Anchor' by Novo Amor

'On Board' by Alana Henderson

'何もきかないで' (Nani mo kikanaide) by Yumi Arai

'Yesterday' by The Beatles

'With or without you' by U2

'Melting' by Cuco

'Change' by Big Thief

'Color Me Blue' by Akane

'Evening Sky' by Austin Farwell

Scan with spotify

www.ingramcontent.com/pod-product-compliance
Lightning Source LLC
Chambersburg PA
CBHW020917160726
47993CB00005B/2020